WITHOUT RESPECT

Mobsters' Gay Sons Series

Book One

BRINA BRADY

Gay Age Gap/Mafia Romance

AUTHOR'S NOTE: This book contains graphic gay sex.

DEDICATION

Thank you to all my awesome Beta Readers for helping me out until I finished my novel. Your help has been invaluable to me, and I don't know how I would have managed without your help and support. Again, thank you so much. I sincerely appreciate your help.

Cj Lewis

Debby Demedicis Elliott

Anita Ford

Anne Michan

Emma King

BRINA BRADY

WITHOUT RESPECT BLURB

An Italian mobster raises three sons, but Sal's youngest son, Benito Banetti, is gay. His father would never permit Ben to be in an openly gay relationship. But Ben intends to change that when he finds the man he wants. When it turns out the man Ben's been seeing is a Banetti family enemy, his father gives him an ultimatum. Either he marries his cousin and all is forgotten, or if he chooses to be with Mishka Chernov, a Russian mobster, he will disown him.

Mishka Chernov took over his family's business out of love and respect for his father; however, he has come to realize he isn't suitable for this top position in the family. Mishka meets a beautiful man at a sleazy bar, and when he finds out who this man is, he still wants him regardless of the problems Ben Banetti would cause his family's business. Mishka wants the same freedom and separation from family business that Ben has.

Without Respect is about two men raised by mob bosses, realizing their families are enemies, but neither is willing to walk away. This story is book one of a MM romance that follows their relationship. It has some D/s and light BDSM elements.

TABLE OF CONTENTS

CHAPTER ONE

Ben

Ben had nothing to lose and everything to gain if he acted on his feelings, regardless of whether his father approved or not. He hadn't known the Russian existed five weeks ago, so it didn't matter if the man ignored him this evening after he'd fucked Ben in the alley every Friday night for the last four weeks. Rejection was possible, but it was unlikely he'd ditch Ben in a horrific, ego-crushing way.

He scanned the room for alternative men he found attractive. Normally, his objective was to find a hot man to fuck him at a club, then leave alone. He never spent an entire night with a man. Ben repeated scanning the club, looking for the Russian every ten minutes; Mr. Perfect finally made his way to the side of the bar where all the Russian gangsters gathered. All other men hung out on the other side.

Ben wanted to know more about the Russian man of few words. He'd spoken very little to the man during the times he'd ended up pressed against the outside wall in the alley with his jeans yanked down; he seemed out of reach for a relationship and certainly anything exclusive. Ben couldn't have a relationship because of who he was, or rather, because of who his father was. His father would never permit Ben to be in an openly gay relationship. Ben intended to change that. He had a right to find a man who would someday love him.

"Stop staring at that guy," his cousin Dante said.

"Don't tell me what to do," Ben said to his cousin. "You're here to make sure no one blows me away, not to monitor who fucks me."

"He looks dangerous. Not to mention, those guys are all Russian mobsters. You shouldn't get involved," Dante warned.

"But it's okay that you work for my father, an Italian mobster, right? Because Italians are better than Russians." Ben was so sick and tired of his family's need to associate exclusively with Italians. According to his father, anyone who wasn't Italian was deemed as unsuitable and an enemy to the Banetti family. None of that ever made sense to Ben.

"He can choose who he wants," Kylan added.

Both of them followed Ben everywhere in the evenings as per his father's order. Mostly they didn't interact with him, staying in the shadows, but tonight they'd decided to drink with him at the Crowbar Club.

Ben eyed the Russian staring at him, the same way he had every Friday night. Each week, he stood beside the same man. Usually, they talked to each other, but everyone seemed to know him and greeted him when he entered. Somehow, this Russian had known Ben was gay. Although the club wasn't exclusively gay, some gays were openly affectionate here and there. The only odd thing here was the Russians standing on the left side of the club. The invisible line separating them from everyone else intrigued Ben. He didn't have the nerve to walk over there, and the man never came to his side. It was just fucking strange.

Ben's stomach growled reminding him he'd forgotten to eat. He looked at his watch and noticed it was time to look at the Russian. They both looked at each other every ten minutes without planning it; it just happened. His gorgeous gray eyes sparkled across the room. He winked when Ben looked at him, which was the sign to meet outside in the alley.

"I'll be back shortly," Ben said.

"Where do you think you're going?" Dante asked like he was so much older than Ben, not the five years he was.

"I said I'll be back. That's all you need to know."

Ben left the area and made his way outside. He walked to the side where they'd met previously. There he was, dressed in a black suit with his tie undone. He was a couple of inches taller than Ben. His dark hair was laced with silver and styled professionally. The man obviously had money, big money, but Ben didn't care since he had his own. He just wanted a good time.

"I want to know your name," the Russian man said.

"Mark. What's your name?"

"Johnny Walker." He rubbed his silver trimmed beard.

"Hi, Johnny." Ben knew that wasn't his real name, the same way he wasn't giving his rightful name. What was he hiding?

He pushed Ben's back against the wall and kissed him. Their cocks rubbed through their clothes, tongues locking while the Russian man's hands stroked his hair. He removed his tie and tied it over Ben's eyes then turned him around so he faced the brick wall. Ben puffed air out, panting, wanting more.

"Place your hands against the wall and keep them there until I tell you to let them down."

Ben lowered his gaze and raised his palms up against the wall jutting his ass out and said, "Yes, sir."

The man unzipped Ben's jeans and pulled them down to his ankles. Ben heard him rip a condom wrapper and the next thing he felt was the pain of his erection forcing its

11

way inside his ass. Knowing the man didn't use lube, or stretch him, Ben had lubed himself in the men's room earlier. The burning was relentless, but he enjoyed it, knowing he would feel good shortly as he pounded Ben hard.

The Russian pulled his cock out and slapped Ben's ass five times. He'd spanked Ben the other times he fucked him, too. The sharp stings turned Ben on more than he wanted to admit to himself. The control the man had over him always left Ben craving more. Their interactions were far too short for his liking.

The Russian aimed his cockhead at Ben's hole again; inching his erection deeper, more urgently, burning him. The stretch felt like it was almost tearing him. He said nothing, just panted. The Russian slipped his hand under Ben's shirt and grabbed his nip rings, twisting them until Ben jerked from pain. The Russian pounded through the soft muscles inside Ben's entrance, smacking his balls against the top of Ben's thighs, which ignited a desperate need in him all over again. He hit Ben's sensitive spot which made him shudder. Ben was rocking in time with him, trying to accept his cock more deeply. He reached around for Ben's leaking erection again, stroking it with his spit. He hammered his hole faster and harder until Ben's head hit the wall, sharp pain shooting through him.

Ben groaned, arching his back, feeling his hard cock deeper inside his ass.

"Uh! Mark, like that?"

"You're going to make me come," Ben gasped the words.

"I like your dick hard and your hole open for me." The Russian slapped his ass a few more times.

"Yes, sir."

"And I want to mark your ass mine."

Ben nodded, liking the idea of belonging to the Russian man.

He rammed his cock in and out with intense force. Ben raised his butt even higher. He heard a growl behind him. Ben was exhausted when the Russian groaned and flooded his condom, setting off his own orgasm, both of them grunting and moaning. Ben's cum had been fucked out of him. The huge dick pounding his butt slowly withdrew, leaving behind an empty ass.

When they finished, the man took off in a black limo. He hadn't said anything to Ben after he threw the used condom into the trash bin. He left Ben alone while he cleaned himself and pulled up his jeans. Ben could still feel the sting on his butt cheeks from the hard slaps the Russian had given him while he viciously fucked him. He had done this before without any meaningful conversation, but this time Ben craved so much more from the man. After the man's silence, he should run and never meet with him again. He'd fucked Ben until his ass was raw, but he wanted his lover to talk to him and maybe hug him. He was no longer content with a quick fucking outside in a dirty alley. He wanted more.

He returned to the club and washed up in the restroom. A blow-up doll had more emotion and life than the man had for him. Something had died inside Ben this time when he was left alone in the alley. He wasn't supposed to get hurt and fisted tears away. After he threw cold water on his face to hide his new pain and rejection, he found Dante and Kylan at a table.

"Hey, are you okay?" Kylan asked.

"I'd like to go to my condo in Wildwood now." Ben hated how well Kylan had read his emotional state of being. He actually cared about him, never making Ben feel like he was just part of his job. Actually, Kylan older than Ben at almost thirty-six, was the closest Ben had come to having a friend.

"At this hour? Why not the condo here in the city?" Dante asked.

"Look, I'll drop you off, Dante, then I'll take him to Wildwood," Kylan said.

"That'll work. You need to stop hooking up with Russians; those fuckers are dangerous. We don't want to find you dead in an alley," Dante said as he sent a message on his phone.

"Don't tell me what to do, Dante."

"Your father hired us to keep you safe. Your behavior is risky and life threatening. You don't let an enemy fuck you outside where anyone can see you."

"Dante, I don't remember asking for your opinion." As he spoke the words, he felt the pain of ending the hookup so abruptly. The man didn't give a damn about him and that hurt like hell. Why was it hurting? He'd hooked up with many men, but this time it was different and he didn't understand why. He had always protected himself emotionally.

"Look, I have a car picking me up, so I'll see you two tomorrow night."

After his cousin left, Ben sat in the back of Kylan's vehicle.

"Want to sit in the front?" Kylan asked.

Ben didn't answer; he jumped out of the SUV and sat in the passenger seat.

"I watched you, Ben. Talk to me."

"About getting fucked?" It didn't even embarrass Ben that Kylan had watched him getting fucked; their relationship was way past that. He accepted Ben and never discussed what he did with men.

"You've let that guy fuck you for weeks now he ignores you inside the club, and when he's done fucking you he just leaves. That can't be all you want."

"It used to be enough, but with this guy, I want him to care about me. You're right, he dumps me after and I hate that."

"I don't live your life, and I understand why you won't settle with one person, but this isn't working. You need more."

"I'm not going to do this again, it hurts too much. Five weeks, not a thanks or anything. I can't do that with him anymore."

"I hope so, but you make the decisions for you. I'm here to keep you safe."

CHAPTER TWO

Ben

Ben climbed ten flights of stairs, then used the elevator for the last two stories to his father's office in New York City. Overheated from wearing a three-piece suit during the summer heat, he welcomed the coolness of the air conditioning inside the building. His stomach contracted, twisting into a knot from his dark thoughts. His palms were sweaty, his nerves fried. All he'd ever desired was to please his father and family, but he never did.

He must have done something wrong for his father to schedule an unexpected meeting to berate him about his indiscretions or punish him in some way. He couldn't think of one thing he'd done that would have made it to his father's desk. At twenty-one, Ben followed the prescribed workout plan, and ate what his father suggested to build muscles and keep healthy. Maybe his cousin had told his father he'd been drunk at a club, but Dante had been drinking with him so that couldn't be it. Thoughts of the Russian man fucking him in the alley invaded his mind.

Dante didn't approve of him hooking up at the club, and had told him so, but he wouldn't dare bring up that a

Russian guy had fucked Ben in an alley near the club, would he? Many of the problems between his father and himself stemmed from his cousin informing his father of his behavior. However, his two older brothers had done their fair share of causing him problems as well.

Ben took a deep breath and knocked on the locked door as he rocked from one foot to the other. What did his father want with him? His stomach dropped to the ground just thinking about it. He adjusted his silk tie to distract himself. Sweat rolled down from his golden-brown hair to his clean-shaven face; he wiped the wetness away with his hand and stared at the door number. He'd rather be anywhere else than here.

Nico, his father's second in command, opened the door with a big smile. "Come in." He stood back allowing Ben to walk into the waiting room. He gave Ben a hug as he had often done.

"Just a warning—your father isn't happy with you." Nico had been working for the family business forever, and also served as Salvatore Banetti's top hit man. He stood as tall as his father did, but was much more muscular and dangerous.

"He never is, is he?" Ben asked, scanning the room for weapons. His father had never been on the right side of the law.

Every wicked character trait of his older brothers, his father excused, but he squashed every attempt Ben made to stand up for himself. He was tired of his father's disapproval and everything he represented. He demanded others worship him like the holy trinity, which was clearly insane. His two brothers were worshipped for everything they did like their father, who had been cruel. Nobody dared question their beliefs.

"Benito, you look so professional. At least he won't bitch about the way you're dressing this time."

"Thanks." Compliments issued from Nico tended to be rare and greatly appreciated. Benito Banetti hated his first name, so he went by Ben, and only his father and Nico insisted on calling him Benito because he was the son of the great Salvatore Banetti, the mob leader of the Italian family in New York City."

"Go in. He's waiting for you." Nico covered his ears with his hands as if he didn't want to hear his employer shouting at his son. At times, Nico had broken up their fights. Ben could always depend on Nico to have his back, and he was grateful for his protection.

"Do you know why he wants me here?"

Nico nodded. "It's best you hear it from him."

"And? Should I be worried?"

"On a scale of one to ten, and ten being the highest level of anger, he's a seven."

"Then maybe I should turn around and get the fuck out of here." Ben told himself he wouldn't allow his father to put him down in any way.

"Go in. I'll be right outside," Nico ordered.

Ben braced for a fierce argument because he was sure the only reason his father had demanded his appearance here and not at his parents' home in New Jersey, was so his mother couldn't intervene. As the unwelcomed sickness in the pit of his stomach refused to leave him, Ben forced himself to open the door to his father's private office.

"It took you long enough to get your ass over here. Did you take a damn bus?" His father stood to greet him. The calm before the storm. He moved closer to Ben, crowding him. He had a way of claiming Ben's personal space and making it his own. He embraced Ben as if he were his possession not his son. Ben didn't understand why his father made him feel so unlikeable and unworthy to be a member of the family. Clearly, his father didn't like him

21

and Ben was never good enough or man enough. Why couldn't he ignore these feelings?

"I drove, and if you check your watch you'll see I'm on time." Ben stepped back from his father, not comfortable with him touching him. "Parking is a bitch here."

"I gave you a pass with a spot. Why didn't you use it?" His father scanned his body up and down with approval.

"I parked across the street." Ben had no plans of ever using his pass. He didn't want any association to his father.

"I see, you're a big shot now and don't need me anymore." His father shook his head in disbelief. "Sit down. We have something to discuss."

His father so easily replaced their conversations with complaints about Ben, nine times out of ten. This meeting would be no different. Why did he bother using the word, discuss? They never had a decent discussion about anything. His father directed his every move, and expected Ben to obey without any input, despite being his age, and Ben's opinion was never asked for or needed.

Ben sat down while his father moved behind the huge desk where he noticed his father's Glock sat among tons of papers. The colors of the gloomy room squeezed the air out of Ben's lungs, the darkness making it absolutely perfect for an execution room. He wondered if Nico or his father had murdered anyone in here, or tortured them. The familiarity of this sort of dismal atmosphere always brought to light the reality of his father's illegal businesses.

"Why don't you brighten up this room?" Ben asked as he inhaled the stench of old cigars. As he spoke, his father straightened the items on his desk, making sure everything was square and properly spaced. On the desktop, he had a phone, a legal-sized lined yellow pad, a translucent Bic pen with a black top, and a big plastic cube with pictures of Ben's mother, their three sons, and their golden retriever.

"I heard you're fucking around with Russians." His father ignored Ben's question, moving straight away to the purpose of their meeting. He never had time for small talk, not even with his youngest son.

"Have you forgotten you married my mother, who is Russian?"

"That's different. Don't go anywhere near the Chernov family."

"What are you talking about?" Ben didn't understand the purpose of the order. What did the Chernov family have to do with him? He wasn't hanging out with anyone from the Chernov family. Well, not that he knew about. Sure, he'd fucked around with some Russian guys at the club, but he didn't know who they were, neither did they know who he was. He went to the club strictly to hook up and leave alone. That fucking Dante must have fed his father this information.

"No more Russian dicks fucking your ass. Is that clear enough?" Salvatore raised his voice.

Ben stood. "I know I'm a disappointment to you because I'm gay, but who fucks me or who I fuck is none of your damn business."

"Benito, I won't tolerate a traitor in the family. Loyalty and respect must be adhered to." His father picked up his Glock and stroked it.

"What are you saying? If I want to be with a Russian, then I'm disloyal to you?" Ben stared at the gun in his father's hand. What the hell was he doing now? He hated gun games.

"If you insist on fucking around with Russians, you'll lose my protection. That means you'll no longer be a Banetti. You'll be dead to me."

His father had gotten out of his chair which could only mean trouble for Ben. He rushed over to where Ben stood, and before he knew what was happening, his father held the gun in his hand to Ben's forehead. He heard the click of the gun being cocked and couldn't believe his father was going

24

to shoot him right in his damn office. The wall clock ticking would be the last sound he heard. His father had done this before to him, but had never followed through with shooting him thankfully. He used it for intimidation, forcing Ben to follow his orders.

"What's the difference if I'm banned from joining the family organization or dead to you?" With a sense of relief, Ben watched his father lower the gun and place it back on his desk.

"Don't disrespect me, Benito." A powerful slap jerked Ben backwards. The crack of skin contacting skin echoed off the walls. Salvatore's palm turned bright red.

Ben blinked as the back of his father's hand struck him next, actually making him take a small step away to lean against the wall to regain his balance. Rubbing the back of his hand along the stinging side of his face then over his mouth, he hoped to erase the pain and humiliation. He shivered from fatigue, and his eyes burned from old cigar smoke. Not wanting to make direct eye contact with his angry father, he gazed at his own hands and feet. *Now he's hitting me. Fucking bastard. Get out of my life.*

"The difference is, I won't stop anyone from taking you out as a Banetti traitor. And that's what you'd be. If you get married, all will be forgiven. Go home and think

25

about your decision. You marry either Marianna, or some other woman, or you continue fucking around with Russian mobsters. Let me know in two days."

"She's my cousin." Ben rolled his eyes.

"Third cousin. I don't give a fuck who you marry, as long as she wears skirts."

Ben moved further away from his father. "I'm only twenty-one. Why now?"

"Because your perverted sexual adventures are way too public and with the wrong people. Keep your gay shit out of public and not in my face."

"Perverted? Now I'm perverted?" The word perverted hit him hard in his heart. It was hopeless for him to think he could outsmart the mobster Salvatore Banetti. He won, no matter what the situation. He hated him for doling out the consequences for disrespecting him. He had to end his relationship with his father and family. But how?

"I made an appointment with Dr. Luciana for you tomorrow for STD testing." He removed an appointment card from his pocket and handed it to Ben.

"I know how to make my own appointment if I need one." Ben put the card in his jacket pocket without looking at it because he had no plans to see the doctor.

"Make sure you go and get tested. Gay men have to be careful and you are not."

Ben nodded, not wanting to engage his father any further. Many times, his father had gone on rants about gay sexual diseases as if straight sexual diseases hadn't existed.

"I want your decision in two days."

"Here or—"

"Our home in New Jersey. You'll tell me after dinner."

"Got it." Ben walked backwards, but his father approached and hugged him as if the last few minutes hadn't happened. Ben tensed up wishing he would stop touching him.

"Listen to me. Russians aren't that great once you're stuck with one." His father patted him on the back. "You look good today. When do you return to work?"

"The end of August."

***

And just like that, Ben's father had him on lockdown with two security guards. Not one, but two. They were sitting on the couch waiting for him when he came home from New York. Apparently, he didn't trust Ben at all after their meeting. He paced back and forth in his Wildwood Beach condo overlooking the Atlantic Ocean as his two protectors watched his every move.

"Ben, sit down already," Kylan ordered. He always looked as if he'd run a mile, a constant tinge of pink under his russet, reddish-brown skin. Not a man Ben could take on at any level and Ben was smart enough not to try. He knew better than pick a fight with a former Jamaican wrestler, who could beat his ass within minutes.

After his father's latest demands, Ben was determined to separate from him and the family, but these two stood in his way. His father had assigned them to be with him twenty-four/seven until he met his parents for dinner. Ben took a seat across from the two men.

Dante, Ben's cousin, teetered on being overweight, but he was as solid as a rock. He thought he was a hotshot, always wearing sunglasses and walking around like a movie star. Dante tolerated Ben; he knew he only pretended to like him. Dante had bullied Ben as a child and made fun of him being gay. How sad was it he trusted Kylan over his own cousin.

"What did you fight about this time?" Kylan asked as he rubbed his shiny, bald head.

"He knows I'm gay, and he's still asking me to marry a woman."

"That's not the reason, and you know it," Dante said.

"Really? So, what's the reason then?" There were days when Ben hated his cousin and today was one of them.

"He knows about that Russian bar you keep hanging out at in the city."

"Why the fuck did you tell my father about the bar?" Ben never mentioned what he had done in the evenings and his father didn't seem interested, but he seemed to be aware of his whereabouts.

"I had to tell him. That's what he's paying me for," his cousin said.

"Fuck you, Dante! Did you know about this, Kylan?" Ben asked.

"No. I wouldn't tell him you let that Russian mobster fuck you. He'd kill all of us," Kylan said.

"I didn't tell him that. I only said Ben hung out in bars where Russian mobsters frequented," Dante said.

"As long as he's walking and talking, keep your mouth shut," Kylan said to Dante. "He's twenty-one and it's time for him to make his own choices."

"You're not family. That's not how it works with the Banetti's." Dante turned to Ben. "Just call him up and tell him you'll get married. Then do what you want after the wedding, like your father has always done."

"Shut up, Dante," Ben said. "I don't want to hear about my father cheating on my mother. I'm not getting married to cheat. I'm going to tell him to fire both of you and that I'm on my own."

"There's something I need to tell you about that man you left with," Kylan said, changing topics.

"What about him? I don't even know his real name," Ben said.

"Every time we go in there, you two shoot stares and send non-verbal communications," Kylan said. "I checked him out. You can never be with him again."

"Who is he?" Dante demanded.

"He said his name was Johnny Walker." Ben clenched his jaw, annoyed that Kylan knew something he didn't yet.

"Don't tell me you believe that?" Kylan asked.

"I don't care what his real name is," Ben said.

"Did you tell him your real name?" Kylan asked.

"No way. I told him my name was Mark. No last name. I'm not stupid."

"No one said you were stupid. You're the most intelligent person in your family. I'm glad they kept you away from the business. You can own the world on your own."

"Are you going to tell me who he is?"

"Later. Not now." Kylan looked at Dante then at Ben, meaning he didn't want Dante to know.

"Who the fuck is he?" Dante asked.

"You don't need to know."

CHAPTER THREE

Mishka

As he waited for his brother, Jasha, thoughts of that young man wearing tight jeans replayed in his mind. Mishka really didn't know much about him. They met at the Crowbar Club, no words exchanged between them inside the club, only their eyes played with each other in the most sensual way. He made no attempt to come closer—they maintained the same distance in the club each time. When Mishka gave him a signal to go outside, he followed him to the alley. This happened five times with little talk. Either he wasn't interested in a relationship, or he was afraid to have one. Who was he? What did he do? He was the most beautiful man Mishka had ever seen and he felt so good. He had a carefree way about himself and didn't seem to worry about things. That's what Mishka wanted for himself, to be free to do as he pleased, but none of that was possible since he'd taken over the family's illegal businesses from his father. Now, he wanted to leave and be free like the adorable stud at the club on Friday night.

He'd go there again Friday and look for him, but this time he wanted to try to get him into the limo. If he agreed to come home with him, he'd be very excited to learn more about the young man who claimed his name was Mark. Of course, he hadn't mentioned his last name, so he must be hiding from someone, or something. It was a good thing Jasha had taken a picture of him and was trying to research who he was. Mishka had to know more.

Jasha found him in a quiet booth towards the back of the bar, away from the front windows. At age twenty-eight, Jasha had grown a beard which flattered him. There was a ten-year difference with Mishka being the older one. For cousins, they didn't look like each other at all. Jasha had brown eyes and Mishka had gray. Mishka stood and they greeted each other with a kiss on both cheeks, then sat down.

"Hey, I don't think you're going to like what I'm going to tell you," Jasha said.

"Why, is he married?"

"No, worse than that." Jasha sighed.

"Tell me."

"You can't have him. He's Sal Banetti's son. His name is Benito but goes by Ben. He doesn't have a social media footprint with his real name. He graduated from Columbia

University with a Master's Degree in Behavioral Science in June. He's working as a research scientist at the university while he works on his doctorate. Lives in a Wildwood Beach condo during the summer and owns another residence in New York City. He's been arrested a few times, but charges were always dismissed. That's all I found out so far."

"A research scientist? That boy didn't look like a research scientist. Are you positive he's not working for the family?"

"Nope. I talked to a few guys about him. One guy said he's brilliant, but Sal doesn't want him working in the family business. No one mentioned he was gay."

"Oh, he's gay. He loved getting his ass fucked. How old is he?" The image of Ben's bare ass ready and waiting for him came to mind.

"He's twenty-one. Too young for you, and he's your enemy's son. He's a no go. If Sal finds out you fucked his son, he'll put a hit on you and declare war on our family. Save yourself a hell of a lot of trouble and forget about him."

Jasha handed the folder over to Mishka. When he opened it, there was a copy of Ben's driver's license. His beautiful smile. He looked so happy and Mishka wanted to feel the way he looked in his picture. "Thanks for the information. I'll decide who I fuck, not you, or anyone."

"Ben is going to fuck things up. Don't say I didn't warn you."

"I know he'll be a problem. He already is. That explains why he didn't say much to me. Get a foot on him so we know where he goes."

"Sure, I'll take care of it."

"I need his phone number."

"It's in the folder."

Mishka looked inside the folder again and found his cell number. He programed it in his second phone—for his social life that he wanted to keep separate from his business.

"So what are you going to do?" Jasha asked.

"I'm going to make him mine, one way or another." Mishka didn't know how he'd make Ben his, but now he had a way to contact him, he had a place to start.

"Just be careful."

"Thanks. So, how is it going with the mules at the clubs?' Mishka wanted to turn all his businesses into legitimate ones. Most of the Chernov men weren't happy with his decision, including his father when he'd told him.

But his father had promised Mishka he could operate it the way he wanted and so he would.

"I'm having trouble at the North Club in Brooklyn. They're not leaving. What do you want to do about it?"

"Let's go over there. I'll talk to Tony and let him know if he doesn't move out, he'll find trouble he'll regret."

"I can take Tony out. That would send a clear message to the Banetti family," Jasha said.

"No one has to fucking die to obey a simple message. He's a Banetti." Mishka worried that Jasha's hate for the Banetti family had risen to a dangerous level. Hopefully, Jasha wouldn't hate Ben.

"Why should that matter? That never bothered you before Ben. Don't tell me you're going to start making decisions based on who you fuck."

"I don't want drugs at my clubs anymore. They can sell in the streets, somewhere else."

Within thirty minutes, they were at the North Club in Brooklyn. They walked into the club where they were greeted with strobe lights flashing across the raised dance floor, as a DJ live-streamed thumping electronic music. For a Thursday night, the club was overflowing with patrons. The bartender sent a red-haired young woman with their drinks.

"Where's Tony?" Mishka asked the girl.

"He's sitting upstairs with a bunch a people, Mr. Chernov."

"Tell him I want to talk to him at the bar."

"Yes, sir." She rushed upstairs.

"Are you going to talk to him here?" Jasha asked.

"Why not?" Mishka drank his vodka with a twist of lime.

"Do you know Tony is Ben's uncle?"

"I hadn't thought about Ben's family tree." Jasha was right, Ben would complicate things, and he didn't even have him yet. He had to make Ben his. He wanted to see Ben in his bed ready to service him every night, but it was more than that. He had paid escorts for sex, but he wanted more.

Tony stood beside Mishka. "You wanted to see me?"

As soon as Tony finished asking his question, people cleared the area around them.

"We told you not to sell in here. Do you need a personal reminder, or maybe something more permanent?" Mishka asked, noting how much he looked like Salvatore Banetti. But he wasn't as sharp as Sal so it was no wonder Tony was working a low-level position in the family

37

business. Mishka could never treat his cousin the way Sal treated his brother.

"I've been here for five years and now you don't want me here? Why do you think it's crowded here? If I leave, all your business will leave. This is good for both of our families."

"My father is no longer in charge. I do things differently. I don't want anyone selling shit in my club. Don't come in here, or any of my other clubs, if you plan on walking out."

"Sal will call you and tell you how it's going to be."

"Get the fuck out of here now while you can still walk."

Tony left, already on his phone.

"That didn't go well," Jasha said.

"No. These changes will take time. Just keep on it."

"Are you taking calls from Sal?"

"Not if I can help it." Sal Banetti was the last person he wanted to speak to. His father hated Sal but he'd made an agreement for them to sell drugs in their clubs. He wasn't sure why his father had agreed to this deal in the first place.

Later that evening, Mishka sat out on his porch, and while he drank his water, decided he would send a text to Ben.

Johnny Walker: *I'm going to make you mine. Save yourself for me.*

Mishka had hoped for a quick response, but Ben seemed to ignore his message. Little did Ben know, this was only the beginning of his pursuit.

A text came in on his business phone. He looked at the name of Sal Banetti. Why couldn't it be his son calling?

CHAPTER FOUR

Ben

Friday at seven o'clock, Kylan delivered Ben to his parents' home. The Banetti's ocean home—an eight-bedroom, five-bathroom house—was hidden behind the greenery along the main road. Ben's grandfather had built the cedar-shingled Cape Cod-style home. For most of the year, his parents lived in their New York condo, but his mother left for their Florida home during the winter months. What his father didn't know or care about was his mother invited her Russian family to stay with her while he stayed in his New York condo. Unfortunately, it was in the same building Ben had his condo, but thankfully on a different floor. Ben liked to spend time at the beach during the summer and sometimes on the weekends to avoid his father.

"Hey, how are you doing back there?" Kaylan asked.

"It's Friday night and I'm on the way to my parents' house for dinner. I'm fucking pissed off. I don't need this shit in my life anymore."

"Stand your ground."

"Are you coming in?"

40

"No. He wants me to wait outside."

"You never told me who the Russian man was."

"I will when you're done in there. I don't want to overload your head."

Ben walked into the house and made his way to the kitchen. His mother ran up to him and wrapped him in her arms. She stood five foot, two inches, and her lilac perfume enveloped him.

"Ben, I'm so happy you're here for dinner." She spoke in Russian.

"Sorry, I haven't been over in a while, but I've been at the beach a lot," Ben replied also in Russian. She loved when they spoke in Russian because no one else knew what they were saying and she thought Ben needed the practice.

"You're not very tanned for a guy who says he's at the beach."

"Well, that's true. I guess I'll visit you in Florida during the winter."

"I wish you would. Remember, I want you happy, so don't let your father destroy who you are. Whatever happens, you're my son, and we'll see each other regardless of any decision made."

"So, he told you what he wants from me?"

"Yes, of course."

41

"I'm not marrying my cousin."

"He's invited her for dinner tonight, so be nice to her."

"What is wrong with him?" Ben rolled his eyes in disbelief. His father was relentless. Why would he marry his cousin to please a father who would never accept him? If it weren't for his mother, he would have moved to California, far away from all of them. He didn't think he could take another minute of this family.

With the sound of the front door opening, his brothers'—Freddie and Carmen—boisterous voices invaded his ears. His father was assembling the forces against him. Did he think he could bully him into a fraudulent marriage? His mother was the only one who supported him.

"Don't you work?" Freddie asked. He was the oldest son and would someday take over.

"Do you?" Ben asked.

"You take too many vacations," Freddie said.

"School is closed, but I guess you wouldn't know that since you never went to college."

Carmen walked in and said, "Stop insulting us. Why do you think your education makes us less smart?"

"Fuck both of you." Ben heard Freddie say he was such a fag as he walked into the living room where his father was sitting in his chair, smoking a cigar.

"I don't know why you invited Marianna to dinner. I'm never going to marry her."

"Are you telling me who to invite to dinner in my own home?"

"I don't care who you invite to *your* home; that's not the point. You're using her to force me into marriage."

"I want your answer after dinner, not now. Get me a glass of wine before you sit down."

Ben went behind the bar and poured wine into two crystal goblets for his father and himself. After he handed his father his wine, he sat on the couch.

"You didn't choose to be my son, I know that, but since you are, there are certain behavioral expectations. You have broken all of them and I want that resolved."

"Do you mean I don't behave the way all the other members of the Banetti family do? I'm the only one who's different from the others? I can't ever live up to your demands." His father meant the fact that he was gay and that behavior had to end, one way or another. So many times, he'd ranted that Ben couldn't be his son. He didn't make gay boys. Lately, he had calmed down about not

43

being his father, though. He'd attended his graduation at Columbia, and Ben had believed he'd finally accepted him, but he'd been wrong. It was clear he'd never accept Ben as his son.

"Why were you speaking in Russian to your mother?"

"Why not? I don't know tons of Russians to practice my Russian with."

"I don't like it. Not in my house."

Ben took a sip of his wine and again wished he wasn't in this family. "So, what are you saying? I can't speak Russian to my Russian mother?"

"Tell me why I never hear you speak Italian?"

"No one in this house speaks Italian, not even you." His father always answered a question with a question when he didn't want to answer.

"You could have taught your brothers, but you didn't."

"They don't want to learn anything from me."

"Speak English in this house."

His mother walked into the room with Marianna. She smiled at Ben. Why was she wearing a red dress and matching high heels? He wasn't impressed, but he felt sorry for her. Everyone in the family tried to marry her off to any single male and they wouldn't rest until she married. They didn't care what she wanted and now they were doing it to

44

Ben. His cousin was twenty-eight and he didn't know why she'd never found anyone. No one asked her if she even wanted a husband.

"Hi, Ben," Marianna said.

"Nice to see you again," Ben said.

"Sit down, Marianna," Ben's father ordered as he stood, poured her a glass of wine, and left them alone.

"Do you know why I'm here?" Marianna asked.

Ben nodded. "You do know I can't marry you, right?"

"I know, but what if we did and did our own thing?" she suggested.

"I can't do that. When I marry, it will be for love and forever, but that can't happen for a number of reasons."

"I'm your third cousin, not your first, you know that?"

"I'm not in love with you and I'm gay. Why would you marry me?"

"I love you as a cousin, not a lover. I guess you don't know… I'm a lesbian. This is why they are trying to marry me off. They don't want us fucking around with the same sex. This way we would shut up both sets of parents and do our own thing. Just think about it."

"My mother isn't in favor of this bullshit, and you shouldn't be either. I didn't know you were gay, too. That's great, but don't let anyone tell you how to live your life. I'd just as soon walk away."

"You can't walk away. They'll kill you."

"I don't think they'll do that; it's all talk. I'm going to live my life the way I want."

"Your father has killed people in the family for less. Why are you so stupid to think he won't get rid of you?" Marianna took a sip of wine.

His mother told them dinner was ready, so together, they walked to the dining room where they were seated beside each other. Ben was glad it wasn't Sunday or he'd be forced to eat a huge Italian meal. Tonight, she'd baked a roast with mashed potatoes and a salad. His father sat at the head of the table; Ben sat on his left and his oldest brother sat to his right.

"Thank you for this great meal. Let's toast to Ben and Marianna. I'd love to see them make beautiful grandchildren for me."

Everyone picked up their wine glasses and said, "Salute."

Ben pushed his chair back and said, "There's no Ben and Marianna. I have nothing more to say about this subject. Thank you for the invite, but I need to leave." He walked to the end of the table and kissed his mother on the cheek. "I love you, Mom."

"Ben, finish your dinner," his father roared.

"I've lost my appetite. I'm done."

His father stood and made his way to Ben. "We need to talk after dinner."

"We have nothing more to talk about. If you can't accept me as I am, then I'm not your son."

"You don't mean that, do you?" Ben's father asked.

"I mean it." Ben made his way to the front door with his father following behind him.

He shoved Ben against the wall, and punched him so hard in the stomach that Ben stumbled backward, reeling from the punch and blocking more punches his father threw. He hadn't expected him to punch him, and certainly not this hard, but he should have. Did he honestly think he'd let him walk out so easily?

"Why the fuck are you punching me?" Ben held his stomach when it became intolerable.

"Don't disrespect me. You'll finish dinner, then we'll talk. You don't walk away from me. Ever."

"Are you going to blow me away if I leave?"

"You're not leaving, get that straight."

"I've made my decision, so there is no reason to discuss it."

Ben saw the next blow coming and blocked him from hitting his face, but his father continued throwing punches. He heard each hit as it landed, saw the blood, felt the impact of fists and feet and knees and elbows. His punching turned into kicking him everywhere he could get at. Another punch knocked the wind out of Ben. As he protected himself from most of the punches, it felt like he would never breathe again. Ben half turned and stepped back toward the door. At that point, he pulled out his gun from inside his jacket and pointed it at his father.

"Don't touch me," Ben shouted.

"Don't point that gun at me unless you're going to use it."

Ben was blinded by his anger and fear combined. "I don't want to use it, but I'm leaving here for good. I've had it with you and everyone else around here."

His father went for Ben's gun, but Ben pointed at the ceiling and shot out the crystal chandelier. The glass splattered all over the ceramic tile.

His two brothers ran to the hallway. "What the fuck is going on in here?"

"Your brother tried to shoot me."

"Why did you allow him to come in the house with a weapon?" Freddie asked.

"I didn't know he'd be so stupid to bring a gun into our home," Carmen said as they both moved forward. Freddie forced the gun out of Ben's hand while Carmen pinned him to the door.

His father's piercing brown eyes squinted with disapproval. "Ben, if you leave now, don't come back. You're dead to me." His voice was lashed with control and coldness, sending chills down Ben's back. The pain in the pit of Ben's stomach refused to leave. He'd fucked up. He couldn't fix this and make it right. Now, if he could just leave without getting shot in the head.

His mother rushed to Ben. "Leave him alone. Both of you leave my house!" she shouted at Freddie and Carmen. They released Ben and looked at their father for his orders.

"All of you get the fuck out of my house," his father shouted at all three of his sons.

Ben kissed his mother and barreled out of the front door and into the passenger seat of Kylan's car. He was never to sit in the front, but this time he would. He needed to be near someone.

"Hey, you okay?" Kylan asked as he started the engine.

49

"No. I almost shot him." Ben was shaking and needed to recover from the gun firing and his father's behavior.

Kylan raised his eyebrows, and said, "You pulled a gun on your father?"

"That's what happened. He wouldn't let me leave."

"You didn't mention you'd brought a gun. I didn't know you had one."

"I always carry one. I'm gay."

"Where is it now?"

"Freddie and Carmen took it from me, the fucking bastards. I hate all of them except my mother."

"Let's have a drink at the pub, then I'll drive you wherever you want."

"Okay. My nerves are shot." Ben stared at his trembling hands. "He's going to put a hit on me."

"No, he's not. He would never do that. No one in the family would respect him if he did. I'm going to shadow you. I won't get in your way. You do whatever. I'll just be around to make sure you're safe."

Kylan's phone buzzed and he handed it to Ben. "Read my message. I'm sure it's your father firing me."

Ben read his father's message.

Salvatore Banetti: *YOU'RE FIRED!*

"Sorry, but he fired you in all caps."

"Thought so, but I know him. He'll call me up tomorrow and ask me to shadow you everywhere. He's pissed he didn't win this round, but he's still in the game. He's not going to hurt you because that would mean he lost."

"They all hate me and would be happy if I died."

"I wouldn't be happy, so stop talking shit." Kylan parked his car.

Once inside, they sat at a small table and ordered beer.

"Did you eat?" Kylan asked.

"Started to, then all hell broke out when my father made a toast to mine and Marianna's children. He makes me cringe. She's my fucking cousin."

"He wants you married because he's looking for a cover for you."

"Cover for what?"

"He doesn't accept you're gay, neither do any of his friends or family. Never will. There's nothing you can do to change him, but you need to live your own life. I stand with your decision to move away from them. You can't live like this."

"It's always been like this, but this is the first time I've felt strong enough to say no. I feel like shit because I pulled my gun on my father though."

51

"And tell me he's never pointed a gun at you?"

"Should I apologize?" Ben didn't feel comfortable with pointing the gun at his father. What if he'd killed him? There was nothing right about what he'd done; he knew it and it wasn't who he was. He certainly didn't want to act like his father in any way.

"Send him a text."

Ben pulled his phone out, and sent a text.

Ben: *I'm sorry about taking out my gun and pointing it at you. I didn't mean to shoot the chandelier. I'll send a check for it.*

Salvatore Banetti: *No problem. That's the first time you behaved like a son of mine should. Maybe you need to take some more shooting lessons.*

"What did he say?" Kylan asked.

"He said, 'No problem. That's the first time you behaved like a son of mine should.'"

"I told you, he's still in the game. You won this round. He's still talking to you and you're not marrying your cousin. Now you can do what you want."

"Hey, you said you'd tell me the Russian's real name."

"The Russian's name is Mishka Chernov."

"No way. He can't be."

"Don't mess around with him."

CHAPTER FIVE

Ben

Ben moved off the boardwalk and walked along the
sand with the water gently sweeping over his toes. The air
smelled of salt and sea spray, invigorating and refreshing
compared to the scents of vehicle fumes and burnt rubber in
the city. The soft waves lapped against the shoreline
creating an intricate pattern along the smooth sand line.
Loud music from the pier rides and games streamed onto
the beach. The water looked dark, but it reflected the
orange and red of the sky.

A few people were wrapped up in blankets and making
out on the sand. He was tired of being alone. All day, he'd
checked his phone to see if anyone in his family contacted
him, but so far none had. He also reread Johnny Walker's
saved text. The guy lied about who he was, used a phony
name and even had a damn phone with his fake name.
Since Kylan had informed him who the Russian was, he
knew there was no way he could be with Mishka Chernov,
even if Kylan hadn't warned him not to go to the Crowbar
again.

When he turned around to walk back to the boardwalk, a man with a baseball cap was walking towards him. As he neared Ben, he noticed that the man was around the same height and build as Mishka Chernov. If it was him, instead of his usual black suit and white shirt, he wore tight dark jeans and a T-shirt. His arms were muscled. But why would a New York Russian mob boss be walking on Wildwood Beach in New Jersey? As he stopped in front of Ben, he immediately knew it definitely was Mishka. Feeling overwhelmed upon seeing the man again, he froze and stared at him the way he had at the Crowbar.

"I know who you are." Mishka's voice was low, masculine and oh so sure of himself.

"And?" Ben figured he must know a hell of a lot more than his name. He'd found him on the beach. How long had he been trailing him?

"And what?" Mishka asked.

"What are you doing here now that you know who I am?" Ben asked.

"Looking for you," Mishka said.

"But why?" Ben didn't know if that was a good thing or not. He wished he could allow Mishka to fuck him one last time. He craved the man, and they were talking which was something Ben had wanted… until he'd found out who he was. Any other person might fear a mob boss locating them in another state, but Mishka traveling here from New York City couldn't be for just a quick fuck in an alley. Hopefully, he wanted Ben, too, but there was one major problem—they couldn't be together.

"You didn't answer my text message."

"I had nothing to say to you." Ben had wanted to answer his message, but he was afraid to get too close to him. He already had feelings he shouldn't have for this man.

"And you didn't show up at the Crowbar last night. I waited for you."

"No, I didn't."

"Why is that?" Mishka stepped closer.

"I think you know why I can't see you anymore."

"You let me fuck you for five weeks in a row. What changed?"

"I know who you are now."

"And I found out you're not who you said you were, either," Mishka said.

"So we're even then."

"We're discussing you, Benjie Banetti."

"Benjie?" Ben laughed.

"I might call you Benjie sometimes. Do you mind?"

"I don't care what you call me. No one has ever called me Benjie before. And I'll call you… Boss Chernov instead of Johnny."

"How about asking me first?"

"What do you want me to call you?"

"Mishka or Sir."

"Sir? Well, that puts an entire new meaning to who you are, doesn't it?" Ben asked.

"And making you my boy would allow me to discipline your bratty behavior."

"Boy? I've never been anyone's boy before."

"And is that something you'd be willing to pursue with me?"

"I can't be anything to you." Ben wanted to be everything to Mishka, but he knew if he dared try, his father would put a hit on him, even though Kylan didn't think he would.

"I want to get to know you. Spend the weekend with me in New York."

"What I want and what I do aren't the same. No. I can't spend any time with you because I know who you are."

"And?"

"And what?"

"I want you to be mine," Mishka said.

"Your what? Your sex slave?" Ben asked.

"Give me one weekend for you to get to know me—the real me."

"I know all about you from my family. There's no mystery about what you do and why."

"Your family's view is slanted. I want you to see me as I am."

"I can't be with you." Ben wouldn't mind seeing Mishka naked at some point and he wanted to go away with him but he couldn't. Ben felt himself giving in to Mishka's words.

"You'll be under my protection. You won't have to fear anything. I'll take you to a hotel in the city. We can get to know each other."

"Protection from who?" Ben snapped out from his images of Mishka standing naked with a hard on for him.

"From your family, if you need it."

"I'd need to take my security guard. I don't go anywhere without him."

"Is he going to watch me fuck you, too?" Mishka's crooked smile hinted at a wild side.

"He already has. He is always around me." Ben shouldn't have said that but it was the truth.

"Will you ride with me to the city?"

"I shouldn't but I will after I pick up some things and my security guard can follow us."

"That's a deal. Meet me in my limo at the Circle K." He pulled Ben closer and silenced him with an unexpected kiss.

Ben had nothing planned this weekend. His family hadn't communicated with him since the dinner fiasco so he wouldn't be seeing them. He needed to get away and why not see what Mishka had to offer? The only problem would be getting Kylan to agree—he had said he wanted to keep Ben safe and not tell him what to do with his life.

He called Kylan and told him to meet him at his condo. When Ben walked into the condo, Kylan was pacing.

"What did you agree to?" Kylan asked, crossing his arms.

"I'm going to spend the weekend with him in a New York hotel room. I told him you have to be there. You can follow his limo."

"This is a mistake, but you need to work this man out of your system. I'm not following his limo. I'll ride with you. We'll rent a car to return."

"Is your overnight bag packed?" Ben wouldn't argue. He was only too glad Kylan had agreed, even though with reservations. Mostly, he was happy his cousin wasn't around this weekend.

"I have one in the guest room. Your father would kill both of us if he knew what you're doing."

"Hey, if you want to cut out, I get it." Ben didn't want to hurt Kylan in anyway. He needed the job.

"There's no way in hell I'd let you go anywhere with that man without me. He's dangerous, but everyone in your family is, too. I just don't know why he wants you."

"Why not? He likes my ass."

"No. It's not about sex. He wants you, and I don't know why. I'm not saying some gay guy wouldn't want you, but he's a mob boss and wrong for you on so many levels."

They made their way to the Circle K and as soon as they approached the waiting limo, the driver opened the door. Ben poked his head inside, and said, "My security guard is riding with us."

"Sure. Why not."

The driver took their overnight bags as they climbed inside the limo. Kylan sat toward the back while Ben sat across from him. Ben introduced Kylan to Mishka.

"Tell me why you're staying at Wildwood Beach?" Mishka asked.

"I live here in the summer because I love the beach and boardwalk."

"What do you drink?"

"Scotch on ice," Ben said.

"That's what your father drinks."

"How do you know that?"

"I just do. Sometimes, I won't be able to answer your questions for security reasons."

"I understand."

"What does Kylan drink?"

"He doesn't drink when he's working, so he'll have a Diet Coke."

Mishka handed Kylan a Diet Coke, then made a drink for Ben.

"Why didn't you stay and talk to me?" Ben asked

"You mean after? I didn't know what to do with you. I didn't know who you were and I needed more information before I could allow myself to stick around."

"Are you always that cold with the men you fuck?"

"Pretty much, but you're different."

"Because of who I am?"

"Not in the way you think. I wanted you from the first day. Once I learned who you were, it complicated what I wanted, but it didn't change how I felt."

"I was about to write you off. I don't like to be dumped after I've been fucked."

"I won't do that to you anymore and no more dirty alleys."

"What if my father finds out?"

"I don't want you worrying, let me take care of this. No one will get hurt so don't think I'll take out someone from your family. Please just give me a chance."

"Right now, my family isn't talking to me."

"Why is that?"

"Gay shit, that's all."

"I'm sorry you have to deal with that shit. Russians are homophobic too, but I was lucky to have the best father in the world."

"Is he dead?"

"No. He's around. I'm in charge now though and he's traveling."

Ben finished his drink and rested his head back. He must have fallen asleep because Mishka was waking him up as the driver carried their bags to the hotel.

Mishka showed Kylan the extra room that was provided with everything he could possibly want.

"Shout if you need me," Kylan said.

"I will. Thanks for being here."

Mishka and Ben left Kylan, shutting the door separating their suites. They sat on the couch together in the living room area, Mishka looking Ben over as if he wanted to peel his clothes off.

"Let's talk about sex," Ben said.

"Sex? I'd rather fuck you, but this weekend is for us to get to know each other."

"Tell me why I should trust you?"

"Did you know your mother is a distant relative to me?"

"No. I had no idea. Do you know her?"

"No. I heard about her from my mother and relatives. I'm telling you this so you can find something in me to trust. Trusting me is the most important thing I want from you."

"I'm here with you, so I'm working on it."

"Yes, you're here but you brought your security guard. You don't trust me completely, do you?"

"I have no reason to trust you, but it's not just you. I never trust any man."

"Have you been in any relationships?"

"No. My father would never allow me, but I'm old enough to make my own decisions."

"Are you open to a relationship?"

63

"I'm afraid of getting hurt, to be honest. The thought of being thrown away after I give a man my heart isn't what I want."

"Give me a chance to make us work. I don't just want to fuck you. It's going to be more than that. But I want your trust, loyalty, and honesty."

"I want that from you too. But you have to know I'm afraid. Tell me what you want from me in our relationship."

"Respect me at all times. Show your loyalty by making me first. If I ask you to do something for your protection, don't question me. There will be consequences for breaking my rules."

"What consequences?"

"I'll whip your bare ass with my belt."

Mishka's phone rang, interrupting their conversation when he answered it.

"This is why I don't want his men in my clubs selling drugs and whores," Mishka responded in Russian. "We have to kill that agreement one way or another."

"Whose men?" Ben asked in English when Mishka had ended the call.

"How did you know what I was talking about?" Mishka asked.

"Simple. I can speak Russian."

"You're full of surprises."

CHAPTER SIX

Mishka

Mishka hoped Ben's fear didn't make him run from him. He had to believe Mishka would ensure his safety. He would do whatever he had to because he wasn't letting Ben out of his sight. There had to be a way to make him stay with him short of kidnapping him and chaining him to his bed. He laughed at the vivid image he'd created because it would make a fun BDSM scene for them later if Ben were into that.

"Follow me," Mishka ordered.

Immediately Ben obeyed his command, which brought a sensual smile to Mishka's lips. Ben stood about a head shorter than Mishka and his golden-brown hair framed his handsome face. Ben had an irresistible charm about him; from his clean-shaven chin to his startlingly intense icy-blue eyes. His nose was perfectly symmetrical, like an aristocrat. The way he dressed and moved denoted he could be a GQ model or Wall Street trader. His enticing lips were slightly full—the kind that end in a cute little smirk at the corners. Mishka figured Ben used his charm to get anything he wanted.

Mishka craved Ben's body but needed his trust more than anything else for them to work. He'd go slow with him and introduce him into his lifestyle; he was positive he'd be a perfect sub. They stood facing each other in the bedroom. Looking at Ben, he couldn't see much resemblance to his father. He didn't look Italian, so he must look more like his Russian mother. Ben's two brothers resembled their father; both had dark hair and eyes. Poor Ben must have been the black sheep of the family, especially since he was gay.

Mishka's father had taken him everywhere as a child, even to meetings with their enemies. He'd trained Mishka to take over when he wanted to retire and travel. That's how he had known Ben's family. Sal Banetti always had his two sons around him and had never mentioned a third son. Mishka hadn't known he existed.

"Strip for me so I can see all of you," Mishka said.

Ben pulled his shirt over his head. "Am I going to see you without your clothes on?"

"Of course, but first I want to see if you can follow my orders in the bedroom. That's important to me."

"Yes, Sir." Ben toyed with his gold nip rings as if he were setting them up for a camera.

"Damn, you're perfect for me."

Among other things, Ben unmercifully teased Mishka, but he made good on it. Mishka was wearing tight jeans, a Columbia University T-shirt, and a gold chain around his neck. He looked at Ben and thought, this guy isn't going anyplace without him.

"Is something wrong with me?" Ben asked.

"Oh no. You're exactly what I've been looking for all these years."

Moments later, Mishka unzipped Ben's jeans and tugged at the waistband, pulling them and his briefs to his knees in one movement. He moved his body, finishing the rest of the job, and then Ben stepped out of them. Ben's naked ass was an open invitation for a punishing paddle. If only he could, but he wasn't ready for that and he hadn't done anything wrong, although he would at some point. He'd have to see if Ben was into that. Everything about him pointed to him loving to take directions from a strong top. He hadn't found many guys who would have allowed Mishka to fuck them in an alley. Ben had said he wouldn't go anywhere with him at the time.

Mishka wanted him so badly and he couldn't explain why. It was much more than lust, but he was beautiful standing there.

"Spread your legs apart."

68

Ben followed his directive without a problem, which delighted Mishka.

"Yes, I wanted to see your balls dangle." Mishka cupped his balls and swung them a bit.

Ben watched him with a close eye, but there was a high interest in what he would do to his balls. "Do you like having your balls touched?"

"I do, Sir." Ben smiled, giving his approval.

"Bend over the back of the chair, stick your ass out, and spread your legs."

Following Mishka's order, Ben moved into position. Mishka knew Ben wanted his cock by the way he stuck his ass up; hopefully, he could stay still and take what he had to give. Already, Ben was making it difficult for him to allow him to leave after the weekend. How could he keep him without forcing or scaring him?

"If I fuck you tonight, it will mean your ass is mine. I don't want you fucking around. Do you have a problem with that?"

"No, Sir. Does that mean you won't fuck anyone else either?"

"I don't want anyone else. I want you. Time will prove that to you." Mishka's cock twitched each time Ben addressed him as Sir.

"Please spank me, Sir," Ben said, running his tongue over his lips.

"If you want me to stop spanking, shout red and I'll stop," Mishka said as his own cock hardened. Ben had no idea what he was doing to Mishka by asking for a spanking first. He'd certainly liked his ass spanked in the alley. What was strange is other men had said similar things, but had never had the same effect on his cock or heart. For some reason, Ben did things to Mishka's body which no other man had.

"Yes, Sir."

Mishka spanked the middle of Ben's white cheeks relentlessly. It must have stung because it had Ben alternately yelping and biting his lip. He continued the hard slaps without stopping for a moment between each one. He enjoyed spanking Ben so much that he lost count of how many times his hand fell on his tight ass. His open palm stung from the hard, repetitive blows. After a couple of minutes of non-stop smacking, his pretty ass cheeks turned red. He tried to wiggle away from Mishka, but couldn't since Mishka rearranged him right back where he wanted him. He waited to see if Ben would tell him to stop with words not body movements, but he didn't.

When he'd finished blistering Ben's ass to a pretty shade of red, Mishka returned to work on his gold nip rings again. How convenient for Mishka that Ben already had nip rings. He was just the right man for him and no other would do. Yet, he would always be a challenge due to who he was and how he acted.

"Your dick is still hard," Mishka said, hoping that was a positive sign he enjoyed spankings.

"That's because I loved what you were doing to me. It connects to my balls and cock. I didn't want you to stop."

"Spanking can be intoxicating, but your ass is red. I can use more than my hand, but not this weekend. We're getting to know each other. I want to fuck you, but we need to take a shower first."

"Yes, Sir."

Ben walked with Mishka into the bathroom. A smile crinkled on Ben's face as if Mishka had given him a gift when Mishka undressed and he figured out they would shower together. Mishka didn't miss Ben staring at his erection and seemed pleased. Of course, he would be. Mishka was proud of the size of his cock and was content that Ben appreciated it, too.

Mishka entered the shower stall, extended his hand out for Ben, and helped him. First, he soaped Ben up and rubbed his cock and balls clean. He labored over washing Ben's golden-brown hair. After he rinsed Ben's hair, Mishka scrubbed Ben's back, wrapped his arms around him, and massaged his cock and balls gently but thoroughly.

"Wash me," Mishka ordered.

Ben washed Mishka's balls and cock first. He used a bar of soap around Mishka's ass area, spending a bit too long there for Mishka's taste. When he did this, Mishka reached around and playfully swatted him on his backside. He slipped the corner of the soap in a little farther than he should have, taking his time.

"Hey, Ben! Is my ass that dirty? That sort of behavior isn't allowed."

"Just cleaning you, Sir." Ben laughed behind Mishka. He continued playing with the soap.

"If you don't get that damn bar of soap out of my ass this minute, you're going to eat it."

Ben withdrew the soap and rinsed Mishka off with the hand shower. He scrubbed his hair and beard, then rinsed them both off.

Mishka pulled the other hand-held shower down, flooding water on Ben's face. Ben stepped back, spraying his showerhead at Mishka. They played, spraying each other until they both were exhausted. Ben brought out the fun side of Mishka that had been hidden for so long. The weight of replacing his father had left little room for fun. Ben was the perfect distraction he needed to rejuvenate himself.

Mishka squeezed Ben's thin waist and swung him around, so he faced the tile. He took the other soap bar and rubbed it between his cheeks to lather his hole up, then stuck his finger inside him and moved it around to give him a stretch. Ben's cock stood at attention as the shower rained down on them. Mishka put on a condom and lubed it up. He'd had one of his men prepare the bathroom for him. Then Mishka leaned over Ben, stuffed his hard cock at the opening, and pushed until he was all in. He slammed his cock in and out of Ben, balls banging, then changed to a slower pace. He continued the pattern while he stroked Ben's cock with his soapy hands. Ben met each thrust as if Mishka had ordered him to please him in that manner. He wasn't a passive bottom, not in any sense of the word.

"I didn't mean to start this now," Mishka said.

"I'm not complaining, Sir. I've never taken a shower with a man before. I like this."

"That's what I like about you. You show your appreciation for my dick in your ass. You get me more than you think." Mishka pulled his cock out of Ben's ass.

"Why did you stop, Sir?" Ben turned around to face him.

"We'll continue this later. I just wanted to tease you a bit."

"Tease me? I want you now." Ben's face strained from sexual frustration.

"You're going to have to wait." Mishka stepped out, threw his condom away in the trashcan, and fetched two large white towels. By then, Ben stood beside him and they dried off before sitting on the bed alongside each other.

Mishka stared into Ben's eyes and smiled. With one hand, he ran his fingers through Ben's damp hair and gently guided his face closer to his, eventually leaning Ben's head on his chest. His other arm wrapped around him, wanting Ben to feel safe with him.

"What hours do you work during the week?" Mishka asked.

"I'm off for two months. Summer vacation."

"Two months without working? And what do you do with all that time?" Mishka asked.

"I travel and hang out at the beach. During the school year, I live in the city."

"What are you doing in school?"

"I'm working on my doctorate degree and work as a professor's assistant."

"What are you studying?"

"Genetics on the research end, with the possibility of teaching at the university level."

"Very impressive for such a young man. I like your lifestyle better than mine. Vacation for two months. Wow."

"I'm spoiled in many ways and I know that. I do charity work during my time off, too."

"Where?"

"I work at a LGBTQ shelter in Brooklyn. I help the boys with school work and help them find jobs."

"I like you even more." Mishka kissed him.

"I'm hungry."

"Want to go out for some Chinese food?"

"Sure." When Ben turned to his side, Mishka slapped his ass. Ben turned his head and looked at him.

"I couldn't resist. I couldn't wait until you were bad."

"Oh, I'm plenty bad."

"Good." Mishka pinched his ass cheek. Ben hadn't flinched when he suggested he would spank him when he was bad. Had he been a sub before?

"I think you like to spank me, don't you?" Ben said.

"Have you ever been to a BDSM club?"

"I've been to a couple of clubs in Europe, but none here. I haven't had much time to get into anything like that since I was working and going to school."

"I thought so. I bet you're a perfect sub."

"And I bet you are a perfect Dom. You have it written all over you. I figured that when you shouted out commands during sex in the alley."

BRINA BRADY

CHAPTER SEVEN

Ben

Ben checked in with Kylan and let him know they were leaving for dinner. He told Ben he'd be around and not to worry. Mishka walked beside Ben without touching him on the crowded sidewalk to the restaurant. Ben hadn't been to Bamboo Dynasty before and was excited to try a new restaurant in the city. When they sauntered inside, delightful smells permeated the air, encouraging a rich appetite. Ben inhaled the various fragrant spices, including garlic, ginger, soy, sherry, onions, and peppers.

A beautiful hostess wearing a red cheongsam escorted them to their booth and handed them black leather jacket menus. Ben noticed the impressive gold-colored framed traditional Chinese folding fans on the walls as they followed her. They stepped up inside the raised private booth, slid the red beaded door curtains separating each booth closed, and sat down. A lit white candle sat on the red tablecloth. Low Chinese music playing in the background trickled through the room.

"Do you have any questions?" Mishka asked as he placed his red napkin on his lap.

"If we try to become an *us*, do I have to swear an oath to you and your mob?" Ben placed his napkin on his lap, too.

"What does that have to do with us?"

"My father makes people swear their allegiance to him before he allows them in his circle."

"Did you swear an allegiance to your father?"

"No. Not in words or on paper. I was born into my family. So, it's expected."

"I see. You won't have anything to do with my businesses. The only loyalty I want is for you to be mine exclusively. I don't want anyone touching you."

The hostess returned to their booth and poured hot tea into both their cups from a vintage Chinese style teapot. She smiled at both of them and left.

"I want to get to know you before I agree to anything," Ben said.

"Oh, you'll get to know me this weekend." Mishka peeked through the beads. "Kylan is sitting behind you. Does he work for you or your father?"

"My father fired him, so I hired him."

"Why?" Mishka's gray eyes widened, sparkling with shock and something else Ben couldn't read.

"Because there was an incident concerning me, and he blamed Kylan for not telling him. Kylan is loyal to me. It's easier this way for both of us."

"And your father doesn't have any other replacement security shadowing you?"

"He probably does. I don't know since we're not talking." Ben hoped his father would have forgotten about him after the incident with the gun. What if he found out he's seeing Mishka? His stomach clenched as a heavy weight settled in his chest. What the hell was he thinking going out in public with Mishka? His father's office was only five blocks from here. He panicked for a moment. Kylan would handle it so all he had to do was relax, but he couldn't. He turned his attention to the menu.

"I have security watching your security and any other security lurking out there," Mishka said, obviously sensing Ben's change in mood.

"Can we take the food back to the hotel?" Ben asked.

"What's wrong?" Mishka reached for Ben's hand across the table and held it firmly as a concerned look covered his face.

Ben banged his head against the back of the booth. "I'm fucking worried."

80

Something was off around him, not anything he could clearly pinpoint, but it was a strong feeling he was in danger. Those damn beaded curtains prevented him from seeing Kylan. Without any reason, a deep terror hit him. He was enjoying Mishka, then he had to bring up his father and his anxiety set in. He heard the words of his cousin Marianna warning him his father had taken out family members for less. This wasn't the first time his father had shunned Ben for disobeying an order, and he always made sure Ben suffered with desperation and fear by their separation. Sitting with Mishka Chernov in public was playing with a dangerous fire, but here he was, out and about with him as if he were a normal man without ties to family thugs. When would he learn he couldn't do as he pleased without paying a high price?

"Look at the menu and tell me what you want. I'll order it and ask them to send it to our room."

Ben didn't read the menu because he couldn't focus. Sweat beaded his forehead. "I want shrimp with lobster sauce, sizzling rice soup, and spring rolls." Ben forced himself to answer and hoped what he'd ordered was somewhere on the menu.

"I'll take care of it. Stay here and I'll be right back."
Mishka took Ben's hand and kissed it. "Are you okay
waiting here?"

Ben nodded. "I'll wait for you."

As soon as Mishka left the booth to order their dinners,
Ben's phone buzzed.

Kylan: *Leave the restaurant from the back NOW.*

Ben: *Got it.*

He never questioned Kylan's orders. That was part of
their agreement when Kylan signed up. He wanted to wait
for Mishka, but he knew he didn't have time. If Kylan
thought Mishka should come, he would've said so. He
knew how to follow orders without question when it had to
do with his safety.

As Ben slid through the beaded door curtain and found
the hallway to the back exit, he saw Mishka at the counter
talking. His heart was pounding, torn between running to
Mishka or Kylan. He pushed the back door open and
scanned the area before he stepped out. Kylan shuffled him
into the back seat of a black car and quickly climbed in
beside him. The windows were darkened so no one could
see inside, but they could see out. Without any hesitation,
the driver raced out of the lot.

"What's happening?" Ben asked, his hands trembling.

"I'm sorry, Ben. We have to hide out for a bit."

"Kylan, what about Mishka?" Ben asked.

"I want you to listen to me without talking. Can you do that?" Kylan had a serious look in his dark eyes which frightened Ben.

"Sure, but you're scaring me."

"Your father's men were following you. I saw them in the restaurant. I don't know what they want, but someone just sent me a text saying your father put a hit on us."

"Fuck! I've caused you to be in trouble now. I'm sorry." Ben's stomach soured from the news of his father's despicable action against them.

"Don't worry about me. My job is to protect you from anyone, including your family. We have to go to a safe place."

"What about Mishka?"

"He's the problem. Sorry, but you can't contact anyone right now. Give me your phone."

"Things were starting to go my way, for the first time in my life, and now everything's turned to shit." Ben handed him the phone. He trusted Kylan with his life and he hardly knew Mishka, but he wanted to finish their weekend. If only they'd stayed in the hotel room, they could have been together, getting to know each other.

"Do you trust me?"

"Of course. I didn't want to leave Mishka, but I know when you tell me to do something, it's for my own good."

"I wanted you to enjoy your weekend. You looked happy and he seemed pleased with you. It's not fair, but I told you Mishka would be trouble. I didn't realize your father would put a hit on us though. I still find it difficult to believe, but the tip was from a reliable source. My job is to protect you, and I can't ignore the text."

"I know. How can we make this go away?" Ben asked, hoping it would be soon so he could return to Mishka. That was if he still wanted him after he'd abandoned him at the restaurant. No one should do that to anyone.

"I don't know if we can. We'll hide out, then I'll ask around and verify if there's really a hit on us."

"Where are we going?" Ben didn't like not knowing where his next destination would be.

"Don't ask. You know the rules. I'm going to take care of you."

Ben leaned his head against the window and wished he was anyone except who he was. He would never have the life he wanted. Mishka would probably think he'd dumped him because he didn't like him. How could he not say anything? But Kylan said to leave and he'd left without any questions.

"Can't you send Mishka a message saying that there were security issues for us?"

"Later, not now. After we get settled in tonight, you can send a message. I hate that this is happening to you, but your family is more of a threat than Mishka is."

"Remember you said you didn't know why Mishka wanted me?"

"That's still in my head, too. Things are going on between the Banetti family and the Chernovs. It has to do with an agreement your father had with Mishka's father. Mishka is trying to break that old agreement within the two families. I'm not sure why or where this will go."

CHAPTER EIGHT

Mishka

After Mishka ordered their meals and told the server to send them to his room, he turned to walk back and noticed the curtain to Kylan's booth was open, and he wasn't sitting at his table. He looked around the room to see if there was any danger, but didn't notice anything except two dark haired men, who looked very Italian, watching him. They were probably Banetti's men watching Ben. He rushed to the booth, slid back the beaded curtain, and found it was empty. Ben was gone. What the hell happened to him? He sent a text to Jasha, who was walking around the restaurant with some of the security.

Mishka: *What happened to Ben?*

Jasha: *Ben and his security left in a dark car from the back. I wrote down the license plates.*

Mishka: *Did you put a car on them?*

Jasha: *Not enough time. We're working on it, but it's a rental car.*

Mishka: *Meet me at my hotel room.*

He sent a text to one of his security cars to pick him up. He waited inside the restaurant while the two Italian men sat down to order, but every now and then he caught them watching him. As soon as the limo driver had doubled parked, Mishka made his way to the back seat. His driver had the window closed. Mishka was upset at himself for taking Ben out to eat. What made him think Sal would allow any type of relationship between him and his son? Sal probably saw it as a betrayal from Ben and a threat from him. What was he thinking? Ben had looked so carefree, and Mishka thought he had the life he wanted. Obviously Ben just dealt with it better than he had. They lived the same life, but Ben did so with great limitations because Sal was not a good father to him.

Mishka took the elevator upstairs to his room—his empty room. He'd had a fun night with Ben planned and now he was gone. He went to the bedroom and looked at Ben's overnight bag. He opened it and smelled his clothes, which reminded him of their time together. Such a short time. He'd get him back, one way or another.

A loud knock on the door interrupted his thoughts. Mishka looked through the peephole and saw Jasha. He let him into the room and they both sat on the padded chairs.

"I want Ben back," Mishka said.

"I know you do, but what are your parameters on how we get him?"

"What do you mean? Bring him to me alive. Don't hurt him."

"So, do you want us to kidnap him at gunpoint?" Jasha asked.

"I don't want him hurt. No guns. Just get him here."

"I have two guys on it. What do you have on his security guard?"

"Kylan Caron is his name. He's from Jamaica. Ben said he used to be a wrestler."

"Is there anyway Kylan removed him for Sal? I assume Sal pays him."

"No. Ben said he pays him and his loyalty is to him, not Sal, and I believe him. If Kylan is still working for Sal without telling Ben, then he fooled all of us. But he was with us here, so I don't know. Kylan and Ben seemed to be tight, but Kylan has the last word when it comes to his protection. Ben wouldn't come with me unless Kylan came, too."

"I have to ask you this, so don't get pissed."

"Ask then."

"Is there a possibility Ben got cold feet about hanging out with you and left with Kylan?"

"I don't know. Everything was going great until I brought up his father, then he looked sick and wanted to return to the hotel room. After I ordered the food for delivery, they were both gone. I should have just left with him right then."

"Sal might have put a hit on him if he thinks he betrayed his family to be with you."

"Sal is a cruel bastard, but no one would do that to their own son," Mishka said.

Jasha received a message, so he stopped to read it. "I got word there were Italian security at the restaurant. Word has it; they put a hit on Ben and his security."

"That's why they left. Kylan must have seen them. I saw them too. The thing is if they were going to blow him away, why didn't they do it?"

There was a loud knock on the door. Mishka checked through the peephole. It was the Chinese delivery. He opened the door and handed the young man a tip.

"Great. Now, we have Chinese. Have some. I can't eat."

"Thanks. Why don't you call Dad?" Jasha asked. "He knows Sal better than you."

"That's a good idea."

Mishka went to the bedroom, sat on the bed, and looked at the towel Ben had been wrapped in. They were just beginning to learn about each other. He'd found the right person for him on so many levels, and now he wasn't here. He punched in his father's emergency personal number.

"Mishka! What's wrong?"

"I'm having problems with Sal Banetti."

"Why?"

"It's complicated. I need to know if Sal would put a hit on his son."

"Which son? He has three."

"The little one. Ben."

"The little gay boy. Please, don't tell me you have your eyes set on him."

"He's twenty-one now. And it's too late for your warning."

"Damn it, Mishka. That isn't one of your brighter moves. Not only would Sal put a hit on his son, he'd put one on you and make war with our family. Why are you doing this?" His father's voice rose.

"All I can say is I want Ben and he's currently somewhere with his security guard. Sal might have put a hit on them both. That can't happen. They're in hiding now. I want you to do whatever you can to find them and bring them to me."

"Do you think I'm God and I can change everything you fuck up? Mishka, this is serious shit. Sal will never accept you being with his son. He doesn't even accept poor Ben as gay. All the Banetti's are homophobic. What do you expect from Italians?"

"I never ask you for much, but I need this favor."

"I'll fly to New York City and see what I can do, but for now you better not go anywhere alone."

"I never do."

"I'm not talking about Jasha. You need big time security. Get on it now." His father ended the call.

Jasha entered the bedroom and crossed his arms. "Is he pissed off?"

"I think so, but he's flying in tomorrow."

"Why?"

"He's going to work on it. That's what he said. You know how he is. He doesn't detail shit."

"Well, we have Chinese food. Come and eat," Jasha said.

"I can't eat right now. I'm going to send him a message. He might still have access to his phone if Kylan didn't remove it."

"If he's good, he wouldn't let him send out any messages."

91

"I'll be out there and we'll talk after I send this text."

"Oh, is it going to be a porno message?" Jasha laughed and left the room.

Johnny Walker: *I want to protect you and Kylan. Tell me what you both need. Anything. I want you back. I know why you had to leave. Call or text me anytime. I miss you. Stay safe. Mishka*

Mishka looked at Ben's things in the bags and it just made everything worse. How could he miss Ben already? His emotions had been tangled into knots since the day he'd met him at the Crowbar. Even the little time they'd spent together meant so much to Mishka. Poor Ben was running for his life because he'd taken a chance to be with him. He went back to the living room where Jasha was.

"Let's eat."

"Did you work on getting rid of Banetti's men in our clubs?" Mishka asked.

"I talked to Freddie Banetti. He said Sal sees no reason to change the agreement Dad made with his family."

"Fuck! Nothing is going right." Mishka was beyond frustrated with the slowness of the changes he wanted to make.

"Your problem is you think you can turn criminal enterprises into legal businesses. It doesn't happen easily and it never happens fast without blood."

"Why is it so difficult to do things the right way? I never should have taken over."

"Don't say that to Dad. He did a lot for you and me. He didn't have to adopt me."

"You're my brother now. I don't like to hear you mention the word adopted. He told me he never regretted adopting you. Your father was his younger brother. We share the same blood."

"And you're my older brother, but I'm worried about your desire to have Ben. I don't see how it can work," Jasha said.

"Sal married a Russian. I don't know why he hates Russians."

CHAPTER NINE

Ben

Ben woke up when the car stopped in front of a small beach house. From the outside, the house looked warm and cozy. It was isolated and painted blue with white trim. White sand surrounded the house with the beach right behind it. The ocean was so close you could hear the waves crashing against the sand.

"Are we staying here?" Ben asked.

"Yes. We have a private beach," Kylan said.

"How are you paying for this?"

"It belongs to a friend who's letting us stay here for as long as we need. Let's go inside."

"We don't have any clothes or food." Ben followed Kylan out of the car before the driver left them in front of the house.

"I took care of it. My friend's maid went shopping for us. I gave her our sizes and what type of food we like." Kylan took a key from under a planter of flowers and opened the door.

"Who's cooking?" Ben asked.

"Me."

"Thanks. I owe you everything." Again, guilt set in because Ben's actions had caused his father to threaten Kylan's life for doing his job.

They walked right into the living room of the tiny house which was decorated in blue, white, and sandy hues. The furniture included one small couch and two padded chairs. The casual wooden coffee table included coastal accessories and stacks of art books. The TV was nailed to the wall opposite the chairs. They could see the balcony outside was equipped with a table and chairs and 2 lounge chairs.

"How many bedrooms?" Ben asked.

"Two. So you'll have your privacy. Each bedroom has a bathroom."

Ben sat down on one of the padded chairs, filled with worry. His heavy sadness was like a black cloud following him around and even in crowded rooms he felt so alone. How could his father put a hit on him? Did his mother know about it? He wanted to call her, but Kylan probably wouldn't allow it.

"We'll get through this. Be patient," Kylan said.

"I need to see my phone. Mishka might have left me a message."

Kylan pulled his phone out and handed it to him. "No making calls or sending messages. We have to find out who our enemies are first. At this point, both the Italians and the Russians are our enemies. I need more information."

As soon as Ben looked at this phone, he saw he had three messages. He clicked on the one from Johnny Walker first because he wanted to hear from Mishka.

Johnny Walker: *I want to protect you and Kylan. Tell me what you both need. Anything. I want you back. I know why you had to leave. Call or text me anytime. I miss you. Stay safe. Mishka*

"Mishka wants to protect both of us. He said he'd help with whatever we need. He knows why I left, and wants me to send him a message," Ben told Kylan.

"Text him you're safe. I'm going to put his number in my phone, then I'm going to destroy yours."

Ben hated the idea of not having a phone especially when his access to Mishka would be cutoff, but Kylan was right. Ben composed a message to Mishka while Kylan stood over him and watched what he wrote.

Ben: *I'm safe right now. I'm really pissed I had to leave you. I want to be with you when things are safe for Kylan and me. Thank you for your offer of help. I miss you, too. Please stay safe.*

Next, Ben read a message from Dante.

Dante: *Where the fuck are you? You were supposed to be at your condo in Wildwood. Where's Kylan? He's missing too. What the fuck is going on? You'd better not see that Russian thug.*

Ben didn't like Dante's text at all. It worried him that his cousin would inform his father where they were so he could kill him. He'd do that for Sal. All for the love of money. He hated Dante now and never wanted to see him again. How dare he send him a message like this, as if Ben was too dumb to realize what he was up to. His loyalty went to his father and never to Ben.

He read the third message from his mother.

Larisa Banetti: *Stay safe. Your father has gone crazy over you being with a Chernov. He sent me away. I'm in Florida now. Don't come to Florida because he has men everywhere looking for you. I know you did what you had to do to say true to yourself, and I don't blame you. You're strong and intelligent. You can win this round with your father, son. I'll say a rosary for you every night to keep you safe. I love you and will miss you. Don't answer this. It's not safe.*

Kylan took the phone and read all three messages. He programmed Mishka's and his mother's numbers into his phone, then stomped on it before carrying the pieces to the kitchen and throwing them in the trash. Ben followed him and checked out the tiny kitchen with granite countertops and tile floors, which was equipped with small and large appliances, dinnerware, and cooking utensils. There was also a washer/dryer in the unit. Kylan opened the refrigerator, took out a bottle of wine, and collected two glasses.

"Let's kill this bottle and then get some sleep. I know this isn't what you were hoping for, but for now it is what it is," Kylan said.

Ben lifted his glass to Kylan and said, "To my best friend and protector."

"To my best friend too. Don't worry, you're safe with me."

Ben drank his wine and scanned Kylan up and down. He was a good-looking man, but he never discussed his girlfriends. Didn't anyone care about him? He must be too busy protecting Ben to have a life.

"Hey, how come you never talk about a girlfriend?"

Kylan smiled at him. "I usually never discuss my personal life when I'm on the job."

"I get that, but I thought we were friends, too, or is that only in my head?"

"We've become good friends over the years, and I care about you more than I should for a client."

"So, tell me something about your girlfriends and where you go with them."

Kylan laughed. "I don't have any girlfriends to talk about. I don't date woman."

"What do you mean you don't date women? Who do you date?"

"I'm more like you. I don't date anyone. I have a few one-night stands."

"Where do you pick them up?"

"I pick them up at bars, like you."

"Which bars?"

"Damn, Ben. What do you really want to know?"

"I just want to know what kind of bars you go to, to hook up. I never see you checking out any chicks when we go to bars."

"That's right. I don't do that when I'm on the job."

"What kind of woman do you hook up with?"

"I don't."

"Oh, you don't care. Any woman will do for the night?"

"I'm gay. I thought you knew that."

Blood pounded in Ben's temples as he absorbed the stunning news. "What the hell? You never told me. I thought you were straight."

"Your father hired me from a gay bar where I was working as a bouncer. He made me an offer to protect you and told me about you. He didn't want some straight guy protecting you. He told me I was perfect for the job because I'd understand you and wouldn't insult your lifestyle."

"He never told me you were gay. Dante didn't either," Ben said.

"Your father told me to shut my mouth about it, especially around Dante."

"I'm shocked by this."

"You've seen me when I'm working. I'm on my best behavior."

"I don't know what to say."

"Get some sleep."

The next day, Ben woke up and took a shower, then found some jean shorts and a T-shirt. He smelled bacon and eggs cooking and went to the kitchen, found the coffee maker, and poured himself a cup of coffee.

"It smells so good in here," Ben said.

"Let's take our plates out to the balcony."

Ben followed Kylan outside and sat at the table. The view of the private beach was beyond beautiful and the sea breeze was refreshing.

"Do you think we're safe here?"

"For now, we are. We'll have to move often so no one finds us."

"Oh, I wanted to stay here. It's so nice. Perfect. I'd like to buy this house."

"It's not for sale," Kylan said.

"How about we hit the beach?"

"Sure."

After breakfast, they walked along the private beach, dipping their feet in the water.

"I never want to leave here," Ben said.

"Tell your boyfriend to buy you a house on the beach," Kylan said.

"I buy my own houses."

Ben was daydreaming about Mishka when all of sudden Kylan tackled him to the sand and covered him. He heard two shots, then Kylan moaned and went limp.

Ben stayed under him until he saw blood on the sand, obviously coming from Kylan. He pushed himself out a little and didn't see anyone around. A bullet had punched its way through Kylan's shoulder, causing a gaping hole in its wake, which quickly filled with blood and gushed out. He was breathing, a pool of blood forming around him and soaking his white T-shirt. Ben removed his shirt and held it over the gaping hole.

Ben pulled out Kylan's phone from his pocket and tapped 911.

"911, what's your emergency?"

"There's been a shooting. I'm at 1212 Beach Lane, Ocean City, New Jersey. He was shot two times."

Within ten minutes, an ambulance drove up to the house and the paramedics came with a stretcher and picked him up.

"Someone shot him. I didn't see who. He threw me onto the sand and covered me with his body. Is he going to be okay?"

"Yes. The shots aren't deep."

"I have to go with him."

As soon as they reached the hospital, they took Kylan to surgery to remove the bullets. Everything had happened too fast. He hadn't seen anyone, but Kylan must have seen someone with a gun. He'd acted so fast that Ben didn't know what was happening. The sound of the gun had told him after he was already under Kylan.

BRINA BRADY

CHAPTER TEN

Mishka

The loud sound of knocking on his door woke Mishka. He put on a pair of jeans, checked the peephole, and saw it was his father, Shurik Chernov. At eight in the morning, his silver hair was styled perfectly, as always. He let his father into his room, and watched as he set a bag he carried on the table. They kissed each other on both cheeks. His father wore a clean white shirt, which was buttoned up fully to support the graceful bow tie he was wearing. Over the shirt, he wore a classy vest with four buttons, adding another layer to the overall look of the suit. The jacket fit him like a glove, a tailored glove. It had a subtle pinstripe pattern which gave the suit an elegant look. He wore a styled hat and still looked like a mob boss.

"Oh, Mishka, I can't believe the mess you're making. Maybe you should consider a vacation with little Ben, away from both families. You're really fucking up my deal with the Banetti family."

"Damn it, Dad. You don't waste any time telling me what a dumb fuck I am. I just woke up."

His father handed Mishka a coffee and bagel with cream cheese he'd brought with him. He had one for himself as well.

"Thanks."

"I didn't mean to criticize you. But Mishka, the world doesn't move at your speed. Take it easy. Everything was going well until you fucked with Sal on two counts. I talked to Sal last night, after you called me."

"What did he say?"

"I reminded him he had a Russian wife, and that he'd made a deal with her family. I asked him to think about how he'd felt during that time, and if he could see my son wanted his son. After fifteen minutes of ranting about gay men, I told him that Ben was his son, just as you're mine. He went quiet for a while."

"Did he put a hit on Ben and Kylan?"

"He wouldn't tell me if he had. Then he changed the subject to his men working in our clubs."

"You didn't."

"I'm not done talking. I told him that if he wanted his men to continue to work in our clubs then he would have to allow Ben to be with you for as long as he wants to be. I also told him to call off the hit on him and his guard."

"Wow. I just really don't want them selling drugs in our clubs."

"You better learn the word compromise. If you don't, nothing good will come of you and our family. Work with it."

"Thanks for helping."

After his father left, his social phone rang and he answered it.

"Hello."

"Mishka! I need your help. Kylan was shot on the beach," Ben said.

"Where are you?"

"I'm at Ocean City Hospital in New Jersey."

"Stay there with him. Don't leave. It'll take me over three hours to get to you. I'll come and stay with you. Please trust me."

"I'm so scared. I think one of my father's men tried to kill me, but Kylan protected me and took the shots," Ben said.

"Kylan is a good man. I'll make sure he's protected when I get there. Please stay in the waiting room and don't move."

"I will. Thanks."

Mishka called his driver and Jasha. The driver picked up Jasha first. Mishka had the bellboy bring all their bags out since he didn't plan on returning. This way he'd be able to return the things Ben and Kylan had left behind. He sat in the back with Jasha.

"Shit went down in such a short period," Jasha said.

"I don't understand it. Dad just said he'd talked to Sal."

"And?"

"I have to agree to keep his men at the clubs if I want his son."

"Will he stop the hit on Ben and his guard?"

"He never answered that question. Dad said Sal wants me to call him in two days with my answer, but then someone tried to take Ben out. Kylan protected him and took the bullets."

"Maybe he wanted to take out Kylan."

"I don't think so. Ben was sure the bullets were meant for him. We don't know. I think we need to talk to Kylan when he's out of surgery."

"We'll need to stay there until Kylan gets out of the hospital," Jasha said.

"Well, they were staying somewhere, but I suppose that place isn't safe anymore."

"I guess not."

As soon as they arrived in the waiting room, Mishka spotted Ben wearing shorts without a shirt.

"Ben needs a shirt," Mishka said. "Could you get him a new one in the guest shop?"

"Sure." Jasha left.

Ben's face was so pale and defeated. He went straight to him. "Ben, how are you?"

"Better, now that you're here. Kylan's in the recovery room. He should be out of there shortly, then he has to stay here for a day or so."

"Have you eaten?"

Ben shook his head. "I didn't want to leave here in case they had news about Kylan."

"Did you talk to the police?" Mishka asked.

"Yes. I didn't see anything, so they took my statement and left."

"Good. The less you say to them the better. We'll find out who did this, but you and Kylan need to accept my protection. That doesn't mean you have to swear your loyalty to me or my family, it just means you'll both be safe with me. I want to take you guys to my home. Will you accept my offer?"

"I want to be with you, but what is the cost for our protection? There's always a price."

"Obey my rules so I can keep you safe. That's it. We don't have to talk about this now. Will you stay with me?"

"I will, but I have to talk to Kylan about it first."

"I understand."

Jasha returned with a new shirt.

"Ben, this is my brother, Jasha. He picked up a shirt for you."

Jasha handed the shirt to Ben.

"Thanks, Jasha." He slipped it over his head.

The doctor entered and approached Ben. "Kylan is in his room and awake. He's looking forward to seeing you. He's in room 202."

"When can he come home?" Ben asked.

"You can pick him up tomorrow afternoon, but he needs to rest and not do any heavy lifting."

"Thank you."

"Let me go in first to check with him, then you can see him in a couple of minutes," Mishka said.

Mishka walked into the room and stood by Kylan's bed.

"Hey, I'm here with Ben. He's waiting outside with my brother and he's safe. I wanted to come in and say thank you for protecting Ben. I owe you my life for keeping him safe. You're a hero in my eyes, and Ben is lucky to have you as his security guard and friend. I want to offer both of you protection, if you'll accept it."

"Is that what Ben wants?"

"He called me for help, but when he comes in here ask him. I'll get him for you. Again, thank you. You're one hell of a man to take a bullet for Ben."

"That's my job, but Ben has become a good friend. I love him like a little brother."

"That's beautiful." Mishka left to get Ben.

BRINA BRADY

CHAPTER ELEVEN

Ben

Ben headed to Kylan's hospital room, but stopped in the doorway almost in tears upon seeing his shoulder bandaged. Kylan waving him in with enthusiasm set Ben's mind at ease. Finding Kylan awake and sitting up in bed made it easier to believe he was going to make it through the shooting. His relaxed gaze roved over his face, noticing he was looking a little out of it from his medication. The good news was Kylan would be okay.

"How do you feel?" Ben sat on the side of the bed.

"I'm numb from the pain killers. Are you okay?" Kylan stroked his hand. "I was so worried about you."

"I'm fine. You're my hero after saving me. Those bullets were meant for me." Ben kissed his forehead. "Thanks for protecting me."

"Those bullets were meant for both of us," Kylan said.

"Did you see who shot you?" Ben asked.

"They were Dante's men, but keep that to yourself," Kylan said.

"Was Dante there?" Ben was upset with the reality of his cousin's men shooting at them. He wasn't assured the order came from Dante alone or his father.

"I don't think so." Kylan lost eye contact with Ben and gazed at his water on the tray as if he might not be telling him everything he had seen during the shooting.

"Do you think my father ordered them to do it?"

"I don't know, Ben. But we can't trust anyone in your family. We have to stay away from all of them."

Mishka entered the room with a vase of colorful tulips and set them on the table. He stood beside Ben. The sweet-smelling scent of flowers cut through the sterilized scent in the room.

"Thank you," Kylan said.

"Again, thank you for saving Ben. You're one hell of a security guard. I've told you I'm offering Ben and you my protection—you both can stay in my home. Will you accept?" Mishka asked.

"Is this what you want, Ben?" Kylan asked.

"Yes. We need help and protection right now," Ben said.

"We accept your generous offer and thank you for your help," Kylan said.

"I'm going to take Ben to a local hotel tonight, then we'll be back in the morning. The doctor said you'll be ready tomorrow afternoon to check out. I don't know if you can make a two-hour ride to New York tomorrow, so we'll rent something local until you're up for the trip."

"I'll have pain pills so I can ride in a limo."

"Fine, then. We'll leave from the hospital. I've hired someone to guard your room until you check out with us. My brother Jasha cleared it with the hospital. Get some rest. We'll be back in the morning," Mishka said.

"Thanks," Kylan said.

Ben touched Kylan's hand. "Thanks again. Stay safe."

The limo driver took them to a hotel on the beach. Jasha had rented his own room and Mishka took Ben to his room with their bags.

"Thanks for bringing our things," Ben said.

"Ben, you should take a shower. You still have blood on your arms."

"Okay."

"I'm going to order something for you to eat and don't disappear from the shower this time." Mishka smiled.

"Not a chance." Ben blew Mishka a kiss.

Mishka hugged him. "I'm so glad Kylan saved you from those bullets."

114

"It's my fault Kylan is in the hospital. If he weren't guarding me, he wouldn't have to be in hiding either."

"Take a shower and we'll talk later," Mishka said.

Ben turned on the water and undressed. He looked into the mirror and saw blood on his arms and legs. He had been so worried about Kylan that he hadn't taken the time to look at himself. He began to feel upset more than dirty looking at Kylan's blood on his body. The water alone didn't rinse the blood away, he scrubbed it away with soap, and even when it was gone, he rescrubbed the area. Kylan came so close to dying and so did he for that matter. When he washed his hair, tears raced down his cheeks. His throat tightened and his lips trembled. His body lost the battle to an onslaught of sobs and tears and he fell to his knees and crouched in the stall corner. He couldn't stop thinking about his father wanting him dead, and his cousin having no problem sending his men to do it. It was no mystery his father never approved of his behavior but he had thought he was proud of Ben's hard work at the university. Apparently, being a perfect student didn't make any difference. He didn't know how long he was in there as the water poured over him, crying into his hands, hiding his face. He no longer had a family and he was truly alone in this world because he attempted to live a full life.

115

Mishka came into the bathroom and turned off the water. "Come out of there before you turn into a fish." Mishka reached out to grab Ben's hand and helped him out of the shower. He wrapped the towel around him and cradled him in his arms. Ben rested his head on his shoulder, hiding his tears.

"Don't worry, Ben. I'm going to take care of you and Kylan."

Ben nodded, unable to talk until he controlled his tears. He was safe in Mishka's arms and never wanted to move away.

"You're going through a rough patch right now. I can't imagine how you must be feeling. It hurts me to see you suffering. I'm here whenever you need me." Mishka led him to the bed, holding him in his arms again and stroking his hair and back. "We can talk about it if you want, or we can talk about something else."

"My father threatened to disown me if I fucked around with a Russian, but I never thought he would want me dead." As Ben heard his own words, a sharp pain went through his chest. He took short shallow breaths to calm down. He was in a total meltdown state in front of the man he wanted to impress. So much for that, his ridiculously sensitive side seized any sense of logic.

"You don't know if he did. I don't think he did and my father doesn't think so either."

"Kylan doesn't know who ordered it. He never thought my father would, but…"

"My father talked to your father today," Mishka said.

"About what?" Ben fisted his tears away when Mishka leaned over and kissed his cheek.

"Get in that bed first. I ordered you a sandwich and Coke."

"Eat in bed?" Ben scrunched his nose at the thought.

"Yes. I want you resting. You've been through a lot today." Mishka carried a tray from the table to the bed and set it on Ben's lap.

"Thanks, Mishka. What did our fathers talk about?" Ben looked at his ham sandwich on Rye, realizing he hadn't had anything since the morning with Kylan.

"I am going to make sure nothing happens to you. My father is working on a deal with your father."

"What exactly were they discussing?"

"You and me being together."

"And how did that go?"

"I don't know yet, but he's going to make an agreement. That's why I don't think your father had anything to do with the hit, but if he did, my father will find out."

"I thought you said your father was retired and traveling."

"He flew in after I called him last night and told him the situation."

"About us?"

"Yes."

"Was he angry?"

"Well, for a minute, then he started working on fixing it for us. He's like that. He's the most supportive father anyone could have. I'm sorry you were stuck with Sal. I never liked him. I used to go to the meetings when my father went to see Sal."

"My relationship with my father is so damn complicated. He provided me with many benefits so I could live a carefree lifestyle and he made sure I had many opportunities to succeed. I never had to work hard if I didn't want to. He handed everything to me—money, cars, condos—anything I wanted or needed. But now, I'm hurt and stunned he'd have me put down like a sick dog for being with you."

"Family is always complicated. He may not have put a hit on you. Do you have any other enemies?"

"Enemies? I don't know." Ben's stomach growled reminding him he had forgotten to eat. He took a bite of his sandwich.

"Don't worry about it."

Ben took a sip of his soda.

"Try to eat. You had a long day," Mishka ordered.

"I'm all fucked about losing my family because I wanted to be with you. Why should it matter who I choose to be with? He'd rather I die than allow me to seek happiness."

"Of course it hurts. He's your father. I'm sorry you're upset. But I'm glad you're with me. I'll make sure you'll never regret your decision." Mishka climbed in beside Ben and hugged him. Then he turned to his side, bent his head and kissed Ben.

"Thanks for being here for me," Ben said.

"Please eat."

Ben bit into his sandwich which ignited his hunger from not eating all day. They ate in silence. Ben was worn out without realizing how tired he was. Once they finished, Mishka removed the trays from the bed and returned to sit up beside Ben.

"I can't believe you're here with me. I've wanted you beside me for a long time. I didn't know how I would make you see how good we could be."

"You're my first real boyfriend."

"I'd better be your only boyfriend."

"Are you jealous?"

"Very."

"Then you don't have anything to worry about. I'd never cheat on you."

"I'm dangerous if you do. So don't fuck with me," Mishka said.

Ben was just getting to know Mishka and here he saw a side of him he hadn't seen before, but he would never cheat on his lover when they had a real relationship.

CHAPTER TWELVE

Ben

The next day they picked up Kylan at the hospital and drove to New York. He slept the entire way. The trip seemed endless and boring, but Mishka entertained him with bits of interesting stories about his trip to Russia. Ben had never been there, but he would love to visit his mother's homeland. She was from Moscow or that's what she had said.

From outside the three-story home, it looked like many families could live there. It had a stucco exterior accented with dark brown trim and was topped with a steeply pitched gabled roof. A huge dark brown fence surrounded the home with a gated entrance. Inside, the second floor had to be smaller than the first, allowing for a large balcony surrounding the second story of the house. One chimney poked out the center of the roof. A well-kept garden, with a grass field and flower patches at the edge of the garden encircled the home. The house was a mansion, bigger than Ben had imagined it would be.

Kylan had his own room on the second floor while he was recovering which he went straight to, took a pain pill and went to bed. He told them he was tired and needed to sleep. Ben figured he wanted to get out of the way. Kylan always placed Ben ahead of himself. That's just how he was.

"What do you want to drink?" Mishka asked as they sat in the kitchen on bar stools.

"Vodka on the rocks with a twist of lime." Ben loved to drink vodka, although sometimes he ordered scotch like his father.

"My father will love you. That's what he drinks."

"Do you think he'll really like me?" Ben couldn't imagine a retired Russian mob boss liking him for any reason.

"Yes, he'll love you like he loves me."

"But I'm the son of his enemy." Ben's father took his enemies, especially the Russians, seriously.

"My father gets along with his enemies. He sees Sal and discusses business. But if you make me happy, he'll double love you."

"Stop. He'll hate me."

"Let's take our drinks to our bedroom. Are you up to some fun?"

"Fun in the bedroom is exactly what I need," Ben said.

Ben followed on Mishka's heels. Pleasantly surprised, Ben sucked in a deep breath when Mishka pushed the French doors wide open into the bedroom, the dark green printed comforter and shams complemented the forest-green painted walls. The four-poster, medieval-style, king-sized bed included four restraint loops. The dark colored wood flaunted the darkness and dungeon-like atmosphere. Apparently, Mishka had played in his bedroom as well. The bed was designed for a king or in Mishka's case, a mob boss. It almost seemed too good to be true for him to be in Mishka's bedroom. He didn't doubt for one minute that he'd made the right decision. It sure beat the dirty alley.

"Strip," Mishka ordered.

Ben took his time and removed his shirt. Mishka moved closer to him to unzip his own jeans and yanked them down.

"Get on your back," Mishka ordered as he unzipped his jeans, dropping them to his shoes in a single movement, revealing his already erect cock.

"Sure thing, Sir," Ben said as he rolled further back on the bed.

Mishka laughed. "You learn fast."

"Of course I do," Ben said.

Mishka put a condom on and rubbed some lube on his erection. "Should I let you enjoy this, or should I let you have a rough time of it?"

"Sir, you'd better make sure I enjoy this." Ben was ready and waiting when he saw Mishka's throbbing erection.

After smearing some lube on Ben's hole, he slipped his finger inside. "Oh, it feels so warm inside."

"Next time, you can cool it off with ice cubes, if you like," Ben said.

"I think I like that idea."

Ben's cock let go a stream of pre-cum as Mishka rolled his legs up and back, causing it to land on his stomach. Mishka spread Ben's legs further apart, kissed his hole, and pulled his ass closer to the edge of the bed. Standing before Ben, he used his fingers to pull at the rings in his already erect nipples. Ben moaned as Mishka's rough fingers and hard nails played with them.

"Are you ready?" he asked, squeezing Ben's nipples, knowing he was enjoying it.

Ben moaned, but not with pain. He was anxious to proceed.

Mishka's phone rang with his father's ring. "Damn it. That's my father calling." He reached for his phone and talked to his father, but mostly he listened.

"My father is here. It's always something that gets in the way of us being alone."

"What does he want?" Ben asked.

"He has information on our situation."

"Should I hide?" Ben trembled with the thought of meeting Mishka's father.

"Hide? You never have to hide from my father or anyone else in my family. You are under my protection. He has information that involves you and he wants to meet you. Get Kylan. He wants to talk to him too."

"When will he be here?"

"I told you he's here now. Better put something on. Sorry. I know you've been through a lot and I wanted to fuck you, but he takes priority right now. He wants to see the man who stole my heart."

Ben quickly dressed in a pair of slacks and a shirt. When he was done, he went to Kylan's room. He was sitting up and playing a game on his phone.

"What are you doing coming in here without knocking?" Kylan asked. "I could have been jacking off."

"Sorry. Mr. Chernov is here and wants to talk to us."

"You mean Shurik Chernov?" Kylan got up and tried to put his jeans on. Ben helped him since he was growling from the pain.

"I don't know his first name. Mishka's father is all I know. Are you going to mention Dante's men?" Ben asked.

"No. Don't say anything about it."

"I won't. I didn't tell Mishka either."

"Keep it that way. We don't have all the facts."

"What about your good source that warned you at the Chinese restaurant that my father put a hit on us?" Ben asked.

"A good source is only as good as he is at the time. Maybe he turned on me. I don't know."

They walked downstairs to the living room. Ben was nervous to meet Mishka's father. The well-dressed man walked into the living room and hugged Mishka. The good relationship showed through in how they immediately connected. His eyes moved toward Ben and Kylan.

"So you're Sal's son Benito. You certainly grew up. I've heard very good things about you."

"Thank you, sir. Mishka told me you're the best father that a son can have."

"It helps to have the best son, too. So, I heard you two had some trouble yesterday in Jersey. What exactly happened?" He directed his question to Ben.

"When we were walking a private beach, Kylan threw me on the sand and covered me with his body. He took two bullets in his shoulder protecting me," Ben said.

"Did you see the shooter, Kylan?" Mr. Chernov asked.

"I saw two shooters. They wore black hoods. Average height. That's when I forced Ben down and covered him. That's all I remember."

"I talked to Sal again today. I actually met him in person for lunch. All of you are to listen without talking."

All three of them nodded. Mishka sat beside Ben and Kylan. His father remained standing.

"Of course, you must know your father is against you being with Mishka. He sees it as a betrayal to the family. However, he made a deal you both need to agree to and sign a document. He'll allow you to be with Mishka, but he'll disown you as his son. And, Mishka, he wants you to retain our previous agreement to work in the clubs without harassment. Both of you must agree for this to happen. If you agree, Benito, you will be under the protection of the Chernovs. No Banetti will threaten you. You'll be able to walk about without fear and the same goes for you, Kylan."

"So my father traded me off for maintaining the Banetti drug dealers in your clubs?" Ben knew about the deal his father had made with the Chernovs. He'd heard him discuss it with his brothers. He knew a lot more than anyone in the family thought.

"Sal said he'll disown you as his son if you decide to stay with Mishka, but he said you already knew that because he warned you about the consequences."

"Mr. Chernov, how come you don't disown your son for being with me?"

"Simple answer. I love my son and I want him to be happy. He told me he wants you, and so that's fine with me. I have no problem with gay men. I'm not homophobic like your father."

"Did you find out who shot Kylan?" Mishka asked.

"Sal said he didn't put a hit on Benito or Kylan. He's looking into who did. So, Mishka do you accept the terms?"

"As much as I hate working with the Banetti family, especially that homophobic Sal, yes I'll accept his demands."

"Sign this document for Sal." Mr. Chernov showed Mishka where to sign.

Mishka signed it and swore under his breath. Ben was surprised how much hate Mishka directed at Ben's father.

"Sal said Kylan is no longer a friend or an employee to the Banetti family. So, when you're well, Mishka will hire you as Benito's security guard. Do you accept the job, Kylan?"

"Yes. Thank you, sir," Kylan responded.

"And, Benito, are you willing to betray your family to be with Mishka?" Mr. Chernov asked.

"I'm staying with Mishka. My father is the one who betrayed me, and I never want to see him again," Ben said.

"Sign this document then." Mr. Chernov pointed to the correct place for Ben to sign.

Ben looked at the words, hating that he'd no longer belong to his family. His heart had broken into so many pieces, but he had to live the life he had chosen for himself, not anyone else's.

"Welcome to the Chernov family. You and Kylan will be protected." He walked over to Ben. "Stand up."

Ben stood. Mr. Chernov hugged him, kissing him on both cheeks. "Make my son happy, Benito, and I'll be happy with you."

"I'll never betray him. Never," Ben said.

"That's what I want to hear." He looked over at his son and smiled. "Excellent choice."

"Dad, just remember he goes by Ben not Benito."

"Okay, Ben. Now, I have three sons. And, Mishka, be good to Ben and Kylan. I think you two will be good for each other. It will keep you out of the dirty bars. This way, you'll both be safe. Take care. I'm going to see Sal and give him the signed documents."

"Thanks, Dad." Mishka hugged his father.

"Thanks, Mr. Chernov," Ben said.

When he left, Ben tried to digest everything that had just happened. He was with Mishka, but he no longer had his family. Both his mother and Kylan had told him he would win this game with his father, but he sure didn't feel like he'd won anything. Yes, he was with Mishka and he wanted a chance to make them work, but not at the expense of his family. But there would never be a happily ever after if he remained under his father's authority. He simply refused to allow him to spread his wings and have a relationship. He knew he was doing what was best, or at least he hoped so.

"Ben, I'd like to talk to you about something in my room," Kylan said.

"Sure."

"Ben, come down here when you're done," Mishka told him.

Ben helped Kylan upstairs to his room. He made sure he got into the bed and under the covers.

"Do you need anything?" Ben asked.

"No. Ben, your father would not do this. Nico wouldn't let him. Your mother wouldn't allow it either. I think Dante wanted us dead. I've never trusted him and I didn't like how he treated me. He talked shit to me about you, and I shut his damn mouth up each time. But I need to know what Dante would get with us out of the way."

"He wanted to work with my brothers and be the third son."

"And my source is going to be toast when I get done with him. He told me your father ordered the hit on us while we were at the Chinese restaurant. He lied to me and for what reason?"

"Don't do anything that will set a storm for you."

"Go enjoy your man downstairs. I'll see what I can find out."

"I will. Let me know if you need anything."

"Mishka gave me his number and told me to text him if I need anything."

"That's good. I need a phone because someone stomped on mine." Ben winked.

"Get out of here."

Ben found Mishka in the living room.

"Sit your cute ass on the chair."

Ben sat down. "Why am I sitting here?"

"Because I want us to discuss our relationship."

"I'm listening." He figured there would be a price to pay for his security.

"I want you and Kylan safe. That's my priority right now. So, there will be times I need to leave the house. Jasha will be here to keep you safe until Kylan heals. Where's your phone?"

"Kylan destroyed it for safety."

"I have a throw away you can use until I get you one."

"I can afford my own phone," Ben said.

"I'm in charge of keeping you safe; I'll make decisions based on your safety."

"Yes, Sir."

"This week, I have to make the rounds at my clubs. I thought we could spend some time at the beach. My father has a private place where we can stay safely. Jasha will stay with Kylan."

"Do I have to stay in the house while you're gone?" Ben asked.

"Until my men look into who shot Kylan, it's not safe for you to leave. Even if your father didn't put the hit, someone else did. You're not safe out yet. I plan to take you on a real vacation away from the East Coast after Kylan is better. I know you wouldn't want to leave him until he's well."

"Thanks. We're very close and I care what happens to him."

"I do have some rules for you."

"Rules like a Dom's rules for a sub?"

"No. You're not my sub. Although, I'd like that at some point in our relationship. We're still getting to know each other, and I'll take some aspects of us slower than others. For now, I have one rule: Respect me at all times. Remember I have the last word between us. If you don't respect me, I'll whip your ass red. But remember, you're not my sub. You're my lover for now."

"You're just looking for a reason to play Dom and spank me."

"Hey, I don't need a reason to spank you since you're under my protection. When I Dom you, I don't play. Well in a way I do, but I want to trust you and for you to trust me before we get into that aspect of the relationship."

"So does that mean you're going to spank Kylan too? He's under your protection."

"No. He's a top." Mishka ran his hand through Ben's hair.

"How do you know that?" Ben asked. How much did Mishka know about them? How long had he been watching them and digging for information? And why was he doing it? Was he looking for another soldier in his family? Ben didn't want anything to do with Mishka's family's businesses. He'd had his fill from his own family's criminal enterprises.

"I had him checked out."

"I didn't know he was gay until after we left the Chinese restaurant."

"Are you interested in Kylan?"

"He's my security guard and best friend." Ben saw Mishka's jealous side coming out. He'd never had anyone in his life care for him enough to be jealous. It wasn't as if he'd had tons of relationships—he hadn't. He'd had hookups because his father wouldn't allow him to be in a gay relationship nor would his brothers. Yet his father had hired Kylan, who was gay and a bouncer in a gay bar. He needed to ask Kylan more about that when the time was right and Mishka wasn't around. He certainly didn't want to stoke Mishka's green eye.

"I trust he hasn't hit on you, or has he?" Mishka's eyes squinted as if he were squeezing the truth out of Ben with them. His loud, booming voice seemingly shook the room. His voice reverberated long after he finished speaking, and he had not heard such a threatening sound from Mishka before.

"Never. He's not interested in me that way."

"Did he really watch me fuck you?" Mishka's voice toned down from before.

"I told you he did. He has to be around me when he is shadowing me." Ben hoped Mishka didn't cause problems for Kylan. He didn't want to have to make a choice between them. There was enough pain being with him because of his father's toxic objections.

"Did you know he used to work in a BDSM club as a bouncer?" Mishka asked.

"He did?" Ben hated when everyone around him knew things he didn't. Kylan didn't mention the bar he'd worked in was a BDSM club. What the hell was his father doing in that kind of club?

"He was the club's spanking master. And yes, he was a Dom."

"What the hell? I wonder why he never told me."

"He probably was told not to, and he's smart not to mix business with sex."

"My father told him not to tell me he was gay. It's like everyone around me has a life but me."

"You're going to have a life with me. In time, we'll go to some clubs if you want, but for now we can't go anywhere unless it's out of the country."

"Can my life here start now? If we're done talking that is. Maybe with you finishing what you started earlier?"

"Oh, you better believe I'm going to do that and because you're a little bratty, I'm going to take you across my knee and spank you again."

Ben felt his face warm from a mixture of delight and embarrassment.

"Jesus, you even blush. You're too damn delicious. Get upstairs."

CHAPTER THIRTEEN

Mishka

Mishka loved the idea of Ben living with him and improving his life; no more lonely days or dirty alleys. As soon as Ben was upstairs, Mishka called his father to see if anything had changed after his meeting with Sal Banetti.

"I knew you would call, but why aren't you paying attention to little Ben?" his father asked.

"Oh, he'll get some of my attention, but waiting is part of the pleasure," Mishka said.

"Too much information," his father laughed. "So you're calling about Sal?"

"Yes. Did you see him again?"

"Yes and his top man Nico. One thing about Nico—he loves Benito, as they both call him. So, here's the deal. Tomorrow you'll need to see Sal with me. We'll meet for lunch at Banetti's Ristorante in Brooklyn to smooth out the deal. He also wants Ben there to clear up something with him."

"I hate that bastard. I don't know if Ben will even go. He thinks his father put a hit on them."

"Sal didn't put a hit on them. He claims he doesn't know who did, but that's one of the reasons he wants Ben there."

"Why is he fucking with Ben? He can tell me what he wants to say to Ben. He won't believe what Sal has to say anyway. He's made up his mind already. Nothing will change for Ben."

"He said the deal is off if you don't bring Ben. Do you remember what I told you about compromising? Start practicing it before you get everyone in our family killed. Got it?"

"I'll bring him. What about Kylan? He's still healing." Mishka knew it wasn't going to be easy to get Ben to attend the meeting. The last thing he had wanted to do was pressure Ben into seeing his father.

"No, he doesn't want Kylan there for some reason," his father said.

"Got it. See you at noon. I love you, Dad."

"I love you too. See you tomorrow with Ben."

Mishka ended the call then climbed the stairs and knocked on Kylan's door.

"Come in," Kylan said.

"How are you doing?"

"Getting better." Kylan set his phone on the end table.

"I talked to my father about his meeting with Sal. He wants to see Ben, my father, and me tomorrow to smooth out the agreement. Sal said he didn't and wouldn't put a hit on Ben or you."

"Interesting. I've known Sal for four years. I never thought he'd hurt Ben. When everything is said and done, he wants Ben safe. He believes that if Ben marries a woman, he'll automatically be safe to walk around in the world without threats. He thinks he can erase Ben's gayness. Sal just doesn't get it."

"Do you think Ben will be safe going to the meeting?" Mishka asked.

"I can go with you guys."

"No. Sal doesn't want you there. But I can have my men shadowing us."

"I want to come and help," Kylan insisted.

"No. You did help when you saved him from the bullets. You need to heal because he'll need you when you're at one hundred percent."

Kylan nodded. "Okay."

"Do you think Ben would make a good sub?" Mishka asked, and watched as Kylan raised his eyebrows in confusion. He knew it was an abrupt change of topic, but if anyone would know, he would.

"I don't know. We've never discussed his sexual kinks. But from what I've seen of him when guarding him, he'd be a bratty sub. He's not as submissive as you might think. Though he might like to be or think he is, he has major control issues. He talks shit to anyone who tries to tell him what to do. His entire life he's had to fight for what he wanted. Those two damn brothers were constantly teasing him and putting him down. Ben is brilliant, and I hope you won't squash all that he has achieved at school."

"I would never do that to him. I can see he's intelligent, but very emotional and sensitive. I'll let you sleep. Jasha will be here tomorrow."

"Thanks, Mishka. Please take care of Ben. He's fragile right now."

"I will."

When Mishka walked into his room, he did a double take. Ben was kneeling naked at the foot of the bed with his head bowed and had placed his hands on his knees.

"Ben! Why are you in the submissive position?"

"I was just trying it out to see if you want to play." Ben stood with an erection that made Mishka's cock twitch.

"You're a little tease. *See what I'm missing* is your game? That's how you play?"

"I like teasing you." Ben flickered his eyelashes.

141

"We'll see about that."

"What's the problem?" Ben asked as if he didn't know what he had done wrong.

"Move the chair to the middle of the floor," Mishka ordered, pointing to the wooden chair with a high back. Ben was going to be so much fun to play with, more than he had ever dreamed.

Ben slowly moved the chair, not dragging it, but carrying it across the room.

Mishka sat down on the chair. "Bend over my knee."

"Why?" Ben shot him a blank look.

"Bad boys are punished for trying to control the bedroom."

"What are you going to do?" Ben asked as if he didn't know.

"Bend over now! I don't like to repeat myself. You'll find out soon enough."

Ben leaned over Mishka's lap, looking so ashamed of himself for trying to seduce Mishka to play in a Dom/sub scene. From day one, Ben must learn he wasn't in charge and any attempt to overthrow the balance of power wasn't going to work.

"Lay your hands flat on the carpet," Mishka barked.

Ben pushed his hands down so they were resting flat. Mishka liked what was going to happen. How could he be so lucky that Ben was so damn playful? But Ben had to pay the price for directing sex in Mishka's bedroom.

Without a warning to Ben, the first slap to his ass cheeks fell hard. Almost immediately, Ben clenched his ass cheeks, waiting for Mishka to strike again. He slammed his hand against Ben's ass with all his strength. Poor Ben moaned and groaned. Mishka continued to wallop his ass. All sorts of sweet noises came from his mouth as he stained his cheeks red with his stinging hand. Ben didn't budge, and his pearly pre-cum dripped on Mishka's thighs.

"Remember you aren't the master director in our bedroom."

"Yes, Sir."

"Don't ever attempt to control the bedroom because I'll beat your ass with my belt."

"I'm sorry, Mishka. I won't ever control the bedroom again."

"Who is in charge around here?" Mishka continued to smack his ass.

"You are, Sir."

"So who decides when we're ready to do a BDSM scene?"

"You do, Sir."

"Who decides when I will fuck you?"

"You do, Sir."

"Remember who is in charge in this house. It's not you. No one manipulates me."

"I won't ever do it again. I'm sorry, Sir," he said.

Mishka forced him to stand then stood up beside him to hold him in his arms. "Tell me why you want to do a scene with me."

"I want you to like me and I really wanted you to play Dom to me."

"I do like you, but you need to understand I won't treat you like my sub. Spanking you or disciplining you for the moment has nothing to do with BDSM. It is me setting boundaries in our relationship."

Ben twisted around so he faced Mishka. "Can I do something to please you, Sir?"

"What do you want to do for me?" Mishka could see Ben hadn't learned his lesson yet. He would have to teach him many times before he got the point.

"Suck and swallow your big bad cock, Sir."

"On your knees," Mishka ordered.

BRINA BRADY

CHAPTER FOURTEEN

Ben

Ben moved from standing to his knees in between Mishka's legs. Ben unzipped Mishka's slacks, pulling his huge, fully erect cock out. He placed his hands behind his back the way he figured Mishka wanted him to do to show his submission. He bowed his head, taking the cock in his mouth. He licked and sucked it as much as he could. Mishka pushed his head down to force him to take more of him. His cock traveled to the back of his throat, almost causing Ben to gag.

Ben knew he had to be perfect at this and not make any mistakes if Mishka were to take him seriously. His sole purpose was to provide Mishka with pleasure. In time, he'd learn Mishka's desires by exploring the grandeur of his dazzling erection. Part of Ben had already decided Mishka's cock would belong to him without ever sharing him with anyone else. His only wish was to fulfill his lover's every sexual, emotional, and physical desires. Mishka pumped his cock in and out hard and fast, then Ben felt the throbbing on his tongue as Mishka shot his load in his mouth. Ben swallowed every drop of it, not wanting to displease his lover in any way or give him cause to get rid of him. He was after all with his family's enemy. He didn't like to think about that too much. The danger and fear of being with his father's enemy actually turned him on in a thrilling way, but he had Kylan on his side. He'd make sure he stayed safe if Mishka tired of him.

"Get on all fours on the bed," Mishka ordered.

"Yes, Sir." Ben loved how Mishka took over everything. Being submissive was a turn-on, more than when he had watched porn on the Internet. It was something he had always been drawn to, but he had no idea how to convey it to anyone, and since he usually hooked up with strangers, he didn't have an opportunity to connect on that level.

Mishka stripped off his clothes in a mad rush, walked over to a drawer to pick up a tube of lube and a condom. He put on the condom; then generously lubed his still rock-hard erection. He rubbed some more around Ben's opening and loaded his fingers with it as he slipped one finger inside Ben's tight hole, causing goosebumps to pop all over Ben's body.

"What's the matter?" Mishka asked.

"It's cold, that's all."

"Your ass is nice and red," Mishka said.

"It stings and feels hot."

"And do you like that?"

"Yes, Sir. It reminds me of the spanking and it gets me all excited again."

"Did you ever get spanked over someone's knee before?" Mishka climbed onto the bed and knelt behind Ben.

"No. Not that I can remember." Ben's discipline at home included lots of shouting, slamming doors, and many time outs in his room. No one ever spanked him.

Mishka dusted his hand along Ben's cheek and down to his neck. He wanted to tell Mishka how much the touch meant, but words were impossible to form. Ben's breath caught in his throat. More than anything, Ben needed this man's bare skin next to his. He feared feeling something for Mishka since he really didn't know him. He knew the man required his submission, but yet he wasn't ready for a sub. Ben wanted to belong to Mishka more than he wanted to avoid the loss of his family. In time, he wondered if he would eventually miss his family.

The tip of Mishka's hard cock head pushed inside about an inch. "Hold on to the headboard tightly, so you're steady."

"Yes, Sir." Ben anticipated so much pleasure when Mishka filled him. He wanted everything from Mishka, not knowing what that meant. He needed Mishka inside of him.

"Relax, Ben. Take some deep breaths." Mishka wrapped his arm around Ben and stroked his cock until it hardened again. "It's going to be good for both of us." He gently inched his cock a little deeper and with that, Ben let out a groan. For no reason, tears flooded Ben's cheeks. He didn't want to cry, but everything was coming to a head, causing him to sob.

Mishka pulled out damn fast. "What's wrong?"

Ben couldn't stop the tears sprinkling his cheeks. He desperately wanted to please Mishka, not act like an emotional drama queen. He hated himself for being so damn emotional. Why did his father hurt him this way? He didn't deserve to be treated this way because he was gay. He went to school, got perfect grades, and never flaunted his preference for the same sex. But because he wanted his own life, his father expelled him. He wasn't so sure his father didn't tell Dante to get rid of him permanently. And Mishka wasn't a sure thing; and at any time he could tire of him and then where would he be? He would have lost his family for nothing, but he couldn't let go of Mishka. That damn man had a hold on him in a way no other had.

Mishka pulled him upright, turned Ben around so he faced him. Mishka looked at him with great concern and brought him to a warm embrace. Ben sank his face onto Mishka's chest for comfort.

"I want to meet your needs," Ben said.

"You'll meet my needs. I'm not worried about that, but I'm concerned that you're upset being here with me." He lifted Ben's face up and wiped his tears. "Did I hurt you or make you feel unsafe?"

"No. I'm just fucked up," Ben said.

"Do you want to stop?"

"No, I need you, but I'm afraid you'll get tired of me."

"Never." Mishka kissed him on the lips. "On all fours!" He helped Ben back down into the position and forced his head to rest on the pillow. He ran his hand along his body, sending chills through Ben in a good way.

Mishka's thick cock stretched his quivering hole farther than he ever thought it could stretch. Ben bit down on the pillow hard; trying to muffle his screams of pleasure and pain as Mishka carefully pushed his big cock into his lubed butt hole.

"That's it, Ben," Mishka said. "Stick that cute little ass in the air. You have the most beautiful pink hole. I could fuck you for hours."

Ben moaned extra loud as Mishka's dirty talk excited him even more. "Mmm." Mishka's cock hitting his prostate felt insanely good. The blood flew to his special spot, causing it to swell and become more sensitive. His cock pounding caused a spark of pleasure to burst through him from inside out. Heat erupted through his groin. That feeling excited him, almost made him crazy. Mishka continued to stroke him. He panted and sweated, quivering from the pleasure inside of him.

"Don't ever stop," Ben blurted out.

"I'll never stop." Mishka wrapped his arm around Ben, stroking his cock with more intensity. Mishka twisted Ben's nip rings with his other hand, bringing moans of pleasure from him. He shifted his hands, holding his smooth balls while the other was pulling the foreskin back as far as possible. The pain and pleasure caused Ben to moan in delight.

"Ahh—you're so good, my beautiful Ben," Mishka said.

Mishka flooded his condom, igniting Ben to spill his load in small quick spurts. Ben made animal grunting sounds as his cum landed in Mishka's hand.

Mishka wrapped his arms around Ben and rocked him. "You're perfect for me. I'll never leave you."

"I hope that's true."

"Ben, trust my words."

CHAPTER FIFTEEN

Ben

Kylan joined them for breakfast. There was a young woman cooking in the kitchen, who Ben hadn't seen before. The Russian maid and cook appeared to be in her late teens or early twenties and full of energy that morning. She spoke English as well as Russian. The young woman had the most beautiful brown eyes. She wore a brown and white uniform and her long hair wrapped up in a bun.

"This is Miss Daria Chernov; she's my cook and maid, but she's also a cousin. She stays in the guesthouse near the pool," Mishka said.

Ben smelled homemade bread baking in the oven.

"Miss Daria has prepared a light meal because Ben and I have a meeting with my father and Sal. She'll make you whatever you want, Kylan."

"What meeting?" Ben asked, wondering why he was just finding out about it.

"Your father, demanded we both attend a lunch to finalize our agreement. My father will be there too."

"I don't want to see him." Ben looked over at Kylan who was instructing Miss Daria how he wanted his eggs cooked. He looked much better today than he had yesterday. The sooner he healed completely, the better. Ben still carried guilt over the shooting because he was convinced they'd wanted him dead.

"Look, I don't like Sal, but my father said we have to go to seal the deal."

"Where's the meeting going to be?" Ben asked.

"Banetti Ristorante."

***

Banetti's Ristorante was an Italian restaurant located in Brooklyn, and there was nothing else like it in the area. The modern, light-leaning Italian food was even more impressive. His father had known Ben loved eating at the family-owned restaurant because his grandfather, Joseph Banetti, was the original owner and cook, who left Ben with many happy memories. He had taught Ben how to prepare Italian food. His grandfather was the complete opposite of his father, more like Mishka's. The man was ahead of his times and he never put Ben down for being gay. Ben had missed him since he passed away two years ago.

The smell of Italian food invaded Ben's nostrils as they neared the front door. Ben was glad he had eaten a light breakfast, but he hoped his father wouldn't upset him, leaving him unable to enjoy the food. Shades of red decorated the beautiful expensive restaurant, paintings of Italian scenery decorated the walls, and classic Italian music played in the background. Ben's cousin Marianna greeted them as they entered the restaurant.

"Hi, Ben." She hugged him and whispered in his ear, "You're very brave. I love you. Stay safe."

"Thank you, Cuz. I love you too."

Ben introduced Mishka to Marianna. She looked at Mishka from head to toe, but didn't smile. She was also part of the Russia phobia like the rest of the family.

"They're set up in the private room." She led them to the private gold room.

"You okay, Ben?" Mishka asked.

"No. I don't want to be here," Ben said.

"I don't either. We'll go to the beach after we're done. It will give us something to look forward to later."

As soon as Ben made his appearance in the private room, he wanted to run. His father and Mishka's father were having a private conversation, but what he hadn't expected was to see Nico, his two brothers, and Dante. Why had they invited them to their luncheon? Wasn't this deal between his father and Mishka's father? Obviously he'd assumed wrong. They took the two empty seats, side by side, but across from their fathers.

Marianna's heals clicked as she entered the room carrying two bottles of red wine. She filled everyone's crystal wine glass. A low Italian opera piped into the room to set the mood.

When they all had their wine glasses filled, Sal stood and said, "Today we celebrate resealing a deal with the Chernovs, but today isn't all celebration. I will lose a son who has chosen to betray me to switch his loyalty to them. Salute."

Glasses clicked and Ben met his father's sad eyes which just about gutted him. He looked over at Dante, who sat there so smugly. So, what was the deal with Dante? Why did he send his men after Kylan and him? He glared at Ben and Mishka with disapproval.

After Sal sat down, he said, "I have something to say to Benito."

Everyone faced Ben, who glared at his father. He was more angry than hurt at this point upon hearing what his father had just announced and prayed for strength. He had to take him on to win the game.

"I heard Kylan was shot, and you were lucky to escape the bullets because of Kylan's superior skills at protecting you. I want to tell you and everyone sitting here, I never called for a hit on you or Kylan. I don't know who did, but Dante is investigating this."

"Dante?" Ben blurted out with anger. "He's a useless ass. I don't trust him to do shit for me."

Mr. Chernov smiled at Ben with approval, and Mishka stroked his thigh under the table.

"Do you have a problem with your cousin?" Sal asked.

"I hate that uneducated motherfucker. You should know he doesn't have my best interests at heart. Actually, it's the opposite. You should know this, but you were always deaf to my words."

"Ben, we're also looking into it," Mr. Chernov said. "Don't worry, we'll find them and they will suffer a harsh death."

"Ben, what the hell is wrong with you?" Dante shouted across the table. "I'm the one who shadowed you for two years with Kylan. Why are you talking shit about me? You were always such a spoiled little drama queen. Everyone has pampered you because you're gay."

"Dante!" Sal shouted. "Please refrain from speaking about Benito in a negative light. As a matter of fact, leave the room."

Dante threw his wine glass against the wall, and left the room.

Freddie, Ben's older brother, said, "Pop, you've spoiled Ben. He has a life of Riley. He disrespects you by his blatant disloyalty to our family so he can have his Russian lover. Let him go. He's no loss to our family."

"Who the fuck cares what you think, Freddie. You're too damn lazy to get your own job, and you're not man enough to be independent from Dad. And you make fun of me? Fuck you, too," Ben shouted.

Carmen, the middle brother, said, "I don't think Ben should be a Banetti anymore either. Disown him for what he has done. He has no respect for anyone but himself. He doesn't know how to work as a family member. Ban him from the family."

"I don't give a fuck what you think, either," Ben shouted as he threw his napkin at his brother. He had no idea they were going to have any input into his father's decision about disowning him.

Nico, Sal's right hand man said, "I think Freddie and Carmen should refrain from such hateful talk of their younger brother. You two never gave Ben a chance so he went on his own and educated himself. He's a success on his own merits. I don't vote Ben out. Let him be who he is and accept his lover into the family as Shurik has."

Nico's words almost brought Ben to tears. "Thank you, Nico."

"Freddie and Carmen, you aren't adding to the solution of the problem here, so leave the room," Sal shouted as he pointed to the door. They both shoved their chairs back and sent death glares at Ben.

Nico shot Ben a look of approval. Whenever there were family arguments, Nico would come between the boys and defend Ben. It was noticeable how much he disliked Freddie and Carmen.

"I'd like to say something," Mr. Chernov said. "I welcome your son Ben into my family. You can vote him out or whatever the fuck you want. He's with us now. If you can't accept him as he is, then you don't deserve him."

"I'd like to add something here," Mishka said. "I've agreed to work with your family in my clubs, though I'd prefer the Banetti family not work there. There's no need to banish Ben because he's with me. Our families can attempt to have a personal relationship as well as a business one."

Marianna and another server carried the hot plates of manicotti to the table. Manicotti happened to be Ben's favorite's dish. Why was his father trying to be nice to him? Once the plates were on the table, Marianna poured more wine into their crystal glasses.

"*Mangia. Mangia.* We'll talk more after we eat," Sal said, ignoring Mishka's attempt to bridge a gap with their two families.

Mishka whispered to Ben, "You did good. I'm so proud of you. Once we're out of here, we'll go to the beach."

His father rolled his eyes when Mishka whispered into Ben's ear. He just couldn't take it that his son was gay. Mishka's father winked at them which Ben thought was so friendly and kind.

After they finished eating, Sal spoke again. "Ben, you still have a chance to admit you were wrong to stay with Shurik's son. All you have to do is say you are sorry for your error, and I'll take you back into the family. You just must never see him again."

"I've already made my decision. It's you who betrayed me. I'm your son and you're throwing me out of the family because you see my relationship with Mishka as disloyal to you. My grandfather—your father—accepted my mother, who is a Russian, into the family. You didn't have to choose between my mother and your family. It's not the betrayal and disloyalty to the Banetti family; it's your blind hate for gay men."

"Then so let it be as it is. I disown you, Benito Banetti. There will be no hits on you or Kylan. Go about your perverted lifestyle without any Banetti family member interactions. We're no longer here for you regardless of your needs." He handed a check to Ben. "That's for Kylan. See that he gets it. He's earned it."

Ben placed it in his pocket. Sometimes, Ben had forgotten his father had been the one who filled his information bank, not awarding his father proper credit for the knowledge he had gleaned. His father hadn't gone to college, but he understood more about the world by experiencing first hand than one could learn spending time reading in a classroom. Ben reminded himself that he'd be nowhere without his father's constant attention and guidance; along with the many opportunities his father had afforded him. But none of that mattered, his father had disowned him and he only hoped the Chernovs would not tire of him.

"You're a pathetic father to Ben, but he has my father to replace you. We'll keep him safe, something your family couldn't," Mishka said.

As Sal got up and left the room, Nico stood to leave but before he did, he turned to Ben and said, "You presented yourself like an intelligent strong man. If you need anything, call me. Stay safe, Ben."

"Thanks, Nico."

"Ben, you're a little lion," Mr. Chernov said. "You stood up for yourself, and I'm proud of you. I know Mishka will have his hands full with you. I like you, Ben Banetti. You're the best Banetti I've met so far."

"Do you know my mother?" Ben asked.

"I do. She and I are distant cousins so we saw each other when the family got together for the holidays."

"She misses her family, but she manages to see them in Florida."

"Yes, Mishka's mother used to visit her before she passed away."

"I'm sorry for your loss." Ben had no idea about Mishka's mother. He had never mentioned her.

"Thank you, Ben. I'll be leaving for Mexico tomorrow, Mishka, but when you decide to go on vacation, call me and I'll return."

"Thanks, Dad. I'm going to take Ben to the beach home."

"That's a great idea."

163

CHAPTER SIXTEEN

Mishka

When they got home, Kylan and Jasha were watching an action movie and eating popcorn on the couch. They seemed to get a long which was a good thing.

"How did it go?" Kylan asked.

"He said he didn't put the hit on us and he wouldn't, but he disowned me anyway. I have something from him for you." Ben handed Kylan an envelope.

"Thanks."

"It's for saving me so he could disown me," Ben said.

"You would have been proud of Ben. He told his brothers and cousin off. His father kicked them out."

"Dante was there?" Kylan looked at Ben.

"Yes, well, he was until my father threw him out of the restaurant. My father hired Dante to investigate the shooting."

"Dante? That's interesting. Why him? He doesn't have any investigative skills."

"I don't know," Ben said.

"It doesn't matter. My father is looking into it. We don't care what Dante has to say," Mishka said.

164

"Nico was there too," Ben told Kylan.

"Nico is always looking out for Ben and makes sure no one hurts him. He's a good man," Kylan added.

"We're going to the beach shortly for two days. Want to come with us?" Mishka asked Kylan and Jasha.

"Yes, let's go with them," Jasha said to Kylan.

"Sure. Ben, can you help get my luggage? I can't fucking lift anything."

They went upstairs, leaving Jasha and Mishka to talk. They had clothes already at the beach house so no packing was needed.

"So what do you think?" Mishka asked.

"About Kylan? He's had an interesting life."

"Do you think he's interested in Ben?" Mishka asked.

"No, I don't get those vibes from him. He cares about him the same way you care about me."

"Good. I wish he'd find someone then I wouldn't worry about him."

Mishka asked the driver to stop and purchase a new phone for Ben as they drove to Long Island. The house was on the sand and away from people and public streets. The family home had five bedrooms so Mishka took the room that used to be his parents', which overlooked the ocean and was away from the others. As Ben put his suitcase in the room, Mishka realized, at some point, they'd have to get his things from his condo. He had enough for a couple of days. Once he gave Mishka the go ahead, he'd send movers to pack up his clothes and personal possessions. He'd bring that up later, not wanting to overwhelm Ben with major decisions right now.

"Wow! This is a beach home," Ben said.

"You're safe here. This is a private beach. You can't drive through the roads unless you have the code. You and Kylan will be okay. Do you still think your father put a hit on you?"

"I don't know, but he pretty much doesn't threaten unless he'll take action. He told me if I decided to be with you, he would disown me. He also told me he wouldn't put a hit on me. So, I guess he's telling the truth."

"He seemed upset to lose you to me. He gave you a chance to change your mind. Are you sure you're okay with your decision?"

"Never been more certain about a decision before."

"I got an idea. I know a BDSM club around here. Would you like to go? We'll be just watching and having a drink. And no, I'm not playing with you there unless you're good."

"Now who is doing the teasing?" Ben asked.

166

"Kylan was right about you."

"What did he say about me?"

"He said you're not submissive and you'd make a bratty sub."

Ben laughed. "And he'd know because he's around me all the time."

"I can't get over he watched me fuck you in the alley."

"Get over it, Mishka. I'm sure he did," Ben said.

"Did you know bad subs get whipped?"

"You mean with a whip?"

"Not necessarily. There are other implements. We'll get to see some if you want to go tonight."

"I want to go, but I'd like you to play with me."

"We'll see how things go, Benjie."

"I thought you had forgotten about calling me Benjie."

"I'll call you Benjie when I feel like it."

When they came inside after swimming at the beach, Jasha had ordered pizza. Mishka invited Jasha and Kylan to the club and they had agreed. He was surprised Jasha wanted to go since he wasn't gay, but he wanted to see what happened in a BDSM club. All four dressed in jeans and wore black T-shirts. Mishka put a black leather strap around Ben's neck.

"That's so nobody touches you in there."

"So, I'll be your sub for the night?"

"Make-believe sub," Mishka said.

"What about Jasha?" Ben asked.

"I don't want anyone bothering me either," Jasha said.

"Do you have another one of those black straps for Jasha?" Kylan asked. "We don't want anyone touching him."

Mishka laughed as he went to his room to find another collar for Jasha. He had to admit he was surprised Jasha had wanted to go in the first place and now he wanted a collar. Of course, Jasha knew nothing of BDSM and had no idea of the significance of a collar.

***

As soon as they walked inside the Red Handcuffs BDSM Club, a man dressed in leather handed Doms red handcuffs and two keychains. Mishka held Ben's hand and led him to the stage area featuring a scene. Most of the clients were dressed in leather and some wore very little. The room smelled like leather and men. He had missed that smell and what it had done for him. He'd love to get Ben into one of those private rooms, but the time wasn't right. Mishka knew Ben didn't trust him completely, or maybe not at all. At the moment, Ben worried about death threats and family rejection. A sub must not only need a Dom, he must trust and respect him. He wasn't sure where Ben's respect level was at since he could be parroting what he had thought Mishka wanted. If anyone could outsmart him, it would be Ben. He was smart and beyond anyone he had met.

Ben turned his attention to Kylan, and immediately looked relieved just knowing he was near him. Ben had been so shocked to learn Kylan had been a Dom and worked in a BDSM club. Mishka could see the strong Dom in Kylan but Ben hadn't.

"How about we handcuff these boys?" Kylan suggested.

"Go ahead, Mishka. I'm okay about it," Ben said.

"Put your hands behind your back, boy," Mishka ordered.

Ben had his hands behind his back with great excitement. Kylan was talking to Jasha. Mishka had no idea what they were saying, but shortly after, Kylan handcuffed Jasha. He always tried new things and tonight he looked like he was having fun with Kylan.

Ben stepped closer to Mishka and said, "Can you scratch my cheek, Sir?"

Only Ben would think of something like that so he planned to be one-step ahead of him. He swatted his backside. He was stunned as that wasn't the cheek he had been talking about.

"He needs the spanking bench," Kylan said. "Are you going to let him get away with that?"

"Kylan, I thought you were on my side," Ben said.

"Oh, I am, Ben. I think you'd like the spanking bench," Kylan said.

"He needs to be put in his place." Mishka took Ben's arm and led him to the bench.

"What are you going to use on me?" Ben asked.

"I should use my belt, but there's a nice paddle on the wall." Mishka pulled it down and sprayed it clean with the shelf disinfectant.

"Why are you spraying it?"

"Because I'm going to paddle your bare ass. I think you earned five swats. Shout red if you want me to stop." Mishka removed the handcuffs and stuffed them in his back pocket.

Kylan and Jasha were standing nearby watching them. A couple of other leather men stopped and watched too.

"Get on there," Mishka ordered.

Ben quickly leaned over the bench. Mishka slipped his hand under Ben, unzipped his jeans and shoved them down to his thighs but made sure his balls were covered.

170

Mishka took a step back and positioned himself for the first swing. "Alright. You've got five swats coming. You're going to count them all out, and thank me after each one. Understood?"

"Yes," Ben said.

"Yes what?" Mishka punctuated his question with the paddle against his ass. He loved that sound.

"Ouch, fuck! Yes, Sir." Mishka could see Ben's fingers itching to rub at his stinging ass, but he knew to keep them in place until they were done.

"Drop your hands over the sides of the bench." Mishka strapped his wrists to the bench noting Ben jerked at the sound of the click.

"Don't move." Mishka secured the straps to his ankles.

Mishka ran his hand gently over his ass. "Are you ready?"

"Yes, Sir." His voice was low and respectful as it should be.

Mishka raised the paddle and brought it down evenly on his bare ass, connecting with a loud smack. Almost immediately, Ben clenched his ass at the same time Mishka felt his cock stretching. *Oh he felt that.* He was pleased Ben didn't worry about publicly displaying his ass which probably meant he had done something similar before.

171

Most new subs were shy about being naked in public, but not Ben. He also didn't mind an open paddling either. He could have said no, but he wanted it all, and he wanted it now. All this was a good sign Ben felt comfortable and safe with him or was it because Kylan was present? Mishka wanted to be the one and only person who made Ben safe. However, this was stupid thinking, knowing he couldn't be with Ben nonstop; they both needed Kylan to protect Ben when Mishka couldn't be around. The thought of leaving Ben home frightened him with the thoughts of many horrible scenarios he had conjured in his mind.

"One, thank you, Sir." Mishka grinned as he heard the thanks, and raised the paddle once more, striking his sweet ass.

Smack!

Mishka heard Ben sucking in his breath just before the paddle landed.

"Two, thank you, Sir." Mishka raised it once more, this time alternating between cheeks with each strike of the paddle.

Smack!

"Three, thank you, Sir." Ben's ass turned slightly pink.

Smack!

"Fuck. Four, thank you, Sir." Ben's ass was turning a nice brighter shade of pink, outlining the paddle strikes against his pale skin.

Smack!

"Five, thank you, Sir." Ben's body went limp, knowing he was done.

"Good boy," Mishka whispered in his ear. "I'm so proud of you."

Mishka unfastened the leather straps from his wrists and ankles. He pulled up Ben's jeans and helped him stand, leading him to the bar area, then ordered them both an ice water with lemon.

"That was a big turn on, Mishka."

"I thought so by your hard-on. Are you okay?"

"Yes, Sir."

Jasha and Kylan had disappeared from their immediate vision, and he had no idea where they were. Hopefully, they were both enjoying themselves. He really wanted Jasha to explore more and find something that made him happy. He stayed home alone, or he hung out with Mishka. He never had a girlfriend or showed any interest in having any relationship. They never discussed relationships in any detail since Jasha didn't like talking about sex.

"I like bondage too," Ben said.

173

"Like what?" Mishka wondered if Ben pretended to know less than he really had. He definitely was no stranger to BDSM. He said he'd only visited clubs in Europe. Interesting.

"Like blindfolds, ropes, and chains."

"Chains? Who knew you were into chains?" Mishka laughed.

"Well, I haven't been chained before but at some point I'd like to be."

"And you need to trust me completely before that happens."

"I do trust you," Ben said.

"No, you don't. You want Kylan around because he is the one you trust."

"Where are Kylan and Jasha?"

"I don't know." Mishka looked around and still didn't see any sign of them.

"Is Jasha gay?"

"Not that I know of. He sure wanted to come here though." Mishka didn't care what Jasha was as long as he was happy. A part of Mishka would be hurt if he didn't confide in him. He must know, of all people, Mishka would understand and be supportive.

"Has he ever dated woman?"

"I don't know what he does, but he spends more time with me than anyone else. We're not free agents like you."

"He doesn't look like you at all."

"Well, my father's brother is Jasha's father. The Italians murdered both of his parents so my father adopted him when he was two and I was twelve. We're cousins but my parents raised us as brothers."

"That's really interesting. I wish my father was more like yours."

"You heard what my father said. He has three sons now and he means it. He has never said that to anyone before except for Jasha."

"Thanks for reminding me of that."

"Let's go check out the open private rooms."

Ben followed him to the long hallway where Mishka stopped at an open window. There was a Dom hooking his sub to the St. Andrew's Cross. The sub was naked but the Dom was completely dressed in leather. He used a feather to tickle the boy's back. He then picked up a whip and lashed from his shoulders to his back and ass. He screamed so loudly they heard him in the hallway. The Dom continued whipping him, painting his body with red lines. The Dom then stroked the boy's cock until he came.

"What do you think of this scene so far?" Mishka asked.

"I don't know about a whip. Have you ever used a whip before?" Ben asked.

"Yes. Many subs don't like whips, but I know how to use it so you don't hurt too much. The thing is, with BDSM you don't start at the top. You work yourself into things. It's a buildup."

Ben turned his head to another room across from them. Mishka saw him cringe slightly and quickly turn his head away. When he looked, he saw a cage sitting empty.

"Do you like the cage?" Mishka asked.

"No. When I was in Germany, a Dom locked me in one. He left me in a room alone and never returned. After five hours of screaming to get out, another Dom found me in there before they closed up. He let me out and took me out to eat and calmed me down."

"Did you know the Dom?" Mishka asked.

"No. I didn't. He asked me if I wanted to play with him for the night. I thought it would be okay since it was a club. They had security around, but none went into the room I was in. That happened last year… I haven't been in another BDSM club until now."

"Does that mean you trusted me not to do that to you?"

"I trust you not to walk away from me when we're playing."

"That's a step in the right direction."

Kylan and Jasha caught up with them.

"Are you guys ready to leave?" Jasha asked.

"Sure. Anytime," Mishka said.

CHAPTER SEVENTEEN

Ben

Sunday night, after two days at the beach, they
returned to Mishka's home. He told Ben he had meetings at
some of his clubs in the city, but he'd be home around
seven for dinner. So, it was just Kylan and Miss Daria left
with him in the house. She was working on cleaning all the
blinds today, so she wasn't around much. Ben used his new
phone to look up some new genetic case studies at
Columbia until Kylan showed up in the living room.

"How's your shoulder?" Ben asked.

"Getting better."

"Why didn't you tell me that you worked in a BDSM
club and that you were a Dom?"

"Why would I tell you personal information like that?
And who told you?"

"Mishka told me. He said he checked you out when he
checked me out. I mean, we could have been talking about
the lifestyle I'm interested in."

"Ben, you never mentioned you were interested in
BDSM. The places you went were gay and regular clubs.
You never ventured into one when I was guarding you."

"I guess I didn't. I had a bad experience in Germany with a Dom."

"Who went with you to Germany?"

"No one. I told my father I was going to Cape Cod for two weeks to meet some friends while you were on vacation in Jamaica. I actually traveled through Europe alone."

"Alone? Are you crazy?" Kylan asked.

"I wanted to get some new experiences without anyone watching me."

"What happened?"

"This Dom asked me if I wanted to play with him. So, I did. He put me in a cage then called me a stupid American and left me alone in the room."

"So, you allowed a stranger, in a foreign country, to lock you in a cage?"

"There were security guards, but they never went into the room I was in until the club closed. A nice Dom took me out to eat so I'd calm down. We fucked around for a week, then I had to go home."

"Don't ever do that again! That bastard could've killed you. I don't understand why you do some of the things you do. I should've taken you to Jamaica with me."

"I know I was stupid. I've learned from my mistakes."

179

"I need to visit a guy today, but don't say anything about it to Mishka."

"Personal or business?"

"Business."

"Can I come?" Ben was dying to get out of the house.

"I'm going to meet with my source."

"Why?"

"Find out why he lied to me about your father putting a hit on us."

"Just because my father didn't own up to it doesn't mean he wasn't a part of it."

"No, Ben. This isn't your father's work. I don't believe he would do that. Dante would though."

"So why don't you talk to Dante?" Ben asked.

"That's not how it works, Ben."

"You need me with you in case something happens. We can call a cab."

"Mishka gave me a set of keys to one of his cars in case I wanted to do something."

"So, let's go then."

"Do you swear not to say anything?" Kylan asked.

"Of course. I'll drive since your shoulder is healing."

"You will wait in the car, do you understand?"

"Whatever you say," Ben said.

It took another thirty minutes for Kylan to get ready. Ben worried Kylan might get hurt during his meeting so he took his gun and hid it inside his hoody. Kylan wasn't himself with his hurt shoulder but Ben knew he'd go with or without him, so he figured he'd go. He drove for an hour then Kylan told him to park behind a garage on a back road. He took off and walked around the house. Ben had no idea who lived there and what would happen.

Ben's phone rang, and seeing it was Mishka, he answered it immediately.

"Where are you?" Mishka asked.

"On an errand with Kylan."

"An errand? I told you to stay home until we find out who put a hit on you and Kylan."

"He had to meet someone, so I'm waiting for him in the car."

"How could he leave you alone in the car while he's talking to someone?" Mishka raised his voice.

"Don't worry. I'm packing a Glock. So, I'll be just fine."

"Do you know how to use it?" Mishka asked, showing he was doubtful about Ben's ability to use a weapon in emergency situations.

"Yes. I took lessons. I've practiced with my brothers at the range since I was twelve. So, yes, I know how to use it if I need to."

"I don't like it. Just another reason to give your ass a good whipping tonight for disobeying me."

"If you say so, Sir." Ben wondered why Mishka didn't trust Kylan or his skills as his security guard, yet he hired him. Well, actually his father had been the one to suggest it. Mishka was adding stress to his relationship with Kylan, and he didn't much care for that at all.

Within minutes, Ben heard a gun going off in the backyard. It was a very sharp sound, followed by a quieter one. The sudden shock of the gun going off made Ben's body tense and his arms and legs stiffened. Terror washed over him, raising the fine hairs on the back of his neck. He steadied his breath and tried to calm the panic within him.

"Ben, what the hell was that loud noise?"

"Fireworks," Ben said.

"Are you okay?" Mishka asked.

"Yes, we'll be home shortly." Ben pulled his gun out, but waited when he saw Kylan running towards the car, then he jumped into the back seat.

"You're in trouble. Call me when you get home," Mishka said.

Ben ended the call without saying anymore to Mishka. He was too worried about Kylan. And why had he heard a gun go off in the yard?

"Drive now! No questions," Kylan said.

"Are you okay?" Ben asked, turning around to make sure Kylan wasn't injured.

"I'm fine. Just drive."

As soon as they got back to Mishka's house, Kylan told Ben his shoulder hurt. He crashed upstairs in his bedroom; his door shut, and never came down again. Ben figured he must have shot whoever was in that house, and that person must have been his good source who turned bad. Killing people wasn't anything new to Ben. Living in the Banetti household, killing and torturing enemies was something that happened. His father hadn't distanced Ban completely from the things they'd done. They assumed they'd protected him from the reality of their gruesome lifestyle by keeping him away from the business. More times than not, Ben had lurked in the background, listening to what they had planned and done. Ben had known Kylan wasn't a non-violent person. He'd lived that way when he lived in Jamaica as a wrestler.

Ben was also aware his father wouldn't have trusted Kylan to guard him if he wasn't able to act fast and be able

183

to kill if he needed to. That was probably what had gone down in the backyard. Whatever he'd found out from his source—he didn't like it. Did he kill him? What if the man wasn't dead? Then he would be able to point his finger at Kylan. He was afraid to ask Kylan if he had killed the man. It wasn't something he would share for many reasons, and Ben understood that as much.

"Ben, would you like an ice coffee?" Miss Daria asked.

"Sure. Thanks." Ben noticed she was wearing a neon green bikini instead of her uniform. Most likely, she had gone swimming in the backyard pool. She'd ditched her bun from the morning and now her hair hung down her back. She didn't look anything like she had earlier. What else did she do with her life besides cleaning and cooking?

She returned with a silver tray and handed him his drink. Whipped cream and one cherry topped the coffee. He licked the cream, and then sipped some of the coffee. It tasted as good as it looked.

"This is really delicious."

"Thank you. I'm glad you like it. Mishka called to let me know he's on his way home. He should be here within fifteen minutes," Miss Daria said.

"Why do you live in the guesthouse and not in here?" Ben asked.

"Mishka wanted me in here, but he needs his privacy. It's easier to have my own place. He tends to walk around naked at times."

"Naked?" Ben laughed at the image of Mishka walking around without clothes.

"Well, he dresses up around the time I cook. During the day, he's gone."

"That's kind of an odd thing to do."

"Yes, I suppose it is. Even Jasha walks around naked. But both of them have been so good to me. I explained I wasn't comfortable with that and preferred to live in the guesthouse. It has everything I need. It's not really small plus I can have overnight guests if I want."

"What part of Russia are you from?" Ben ran over the words *overnight guests*. He wondered where she had met these men to bring home to a Russian mobster's home. She either didn't mention it or she didn't know what Mishka did for money.

"Moscow. The only way for me to become an American citizen was for Mishka to adopt me legally, which he did."

"I'd like to speak to you in Russian if you don't mind," Ben said.

"Oh, I didn't know you knew Russian. Anytime we can speak Russian," she said in Russian.

"My mother is Russian and she taught me, but I also took classes." And just like that they were speaking Russian.

CHAPTER EIGHTEEN

Ben

Within a few minutes, Mishka removed his black Patton leather shoes in the foyer on a shoe tray, then he made his way to the living room. He radiated an air of quiet confidence, but Ben detected a slight arrogance in his demeanor. He was wearing an Armani gray pinstripe suit, sharp looking, and well fitted. There were no visible wrinkles anywhere on his clothing. His power suit was exactly the sort of thing that an attorney would wear in court, but Mishka was far from working in a legitimate place of work. Still, it fit well, it made him look very handsome, and when he smiled, it was a little bit magical.

He kissed Miss Daria then kissed Ben.

"I'm roasting a chicken with homemade gravy for dinner. I hope you like that, Ben."

"I love roasted chicken with gravy."

She left them alone and made her way to the kitchen.

"Where's Kylan?" Mishka asked.

"He's been in his room since we got back." Ben noticed his satin silver tie brought out his gray eyes.

"What went down?" Mishka asked.

188

"Nothing."

"Don't lie to me. You left the house with Kylan when I told you to stay home until we solve who put a hit on you. I clearly heard gunshots, and you said it was fireworks. I can't deal with blatant lying. You don't have to swear your allegiance to my family, but you do owe me the respect and loyalty as your lover. And that means to be honest at all times with me." Mishka's voice was full of anger.

"You're asking me to betray Kylan. I can't do that. If you want to know something about him, ask him."

"I see how that goes. Kylan comes first." Mishka picked up Ben's empty cup and threw it against the wall. "That's what I think of you putting Kylan first."

Kylan appeared in the room and stood by Ben. "Hey, if you want to know what's going on with me, don't ask Ben."

"I don't want Ben to leave this house until we find the shooters."

"Ben is and has been my top priority and he will always be safe with me."

"I didn't give you permission to take Ben out of here. If you want to risk your life, do it without involving Ben."

"He drove me to one of my sources. I wanted to see if he had more information."

189

"What did you find out?" Mishka asked.

"The hit came from a Banetti, but not Ben's immediate family."

"Did you have to go in person to find that out?" Mishka asked.

"Yes, I had to find out if and why my source had lied to me."

"Can we both share information for the safety of Ben? You know shit that we need to know to stop them from doing it again."

"My source was bad. He lied to me, but in the end, he told me who ordered the hit. I'll handle it from here," Kylan said.

"Who the fuck was it?" Mishka demanded.

"I'll handle it. It's personal," Kylan said.

"I offered you protection in my home. Then you had the fucking audacity to remove Ben from my home without my permission and put his life at risk. Don't ever take Ben anywhere without my permission. He is under my protection. And now you want to fuck me out of information that affects Ben." Mishka raised his voice, causing Ben to jump. He had never seen Mishka so angry, and it frightened him. It was his father all over again; the anger, possessiveness, and power playing.

190

"Ben's father always entrusted me with him, and I never needed permission. Next time, I'll inform you if I want to take Ben out with me. As far as who put the hit on us, I'd rather discuss this in detail without Ben around."

"Kylan! Tell me. I need to know who did this," Ben shouted.

"I don't want to cause a family war with both families, but I'm going to inform Mishka and he can tell you if he thinks it's okay," Kylan said.

"We'll talk at eight in my study. It's the room down the hall on the left," Mishka said.

Kylan left the room and went upstairs.

"Follow me," Mishka ordered.

Ben had a feeling this was going to be a lesson he'd never forget. He knew Mishka was jealous of Kylan—he wanted Ben only for himself. For some reason, the possibility of Kylan interrupting their relationship threatened Mishka.

They walked and walked through the house until he opened the tall double doors into this distant wing of the house. There were separate doors down the hallway. Why did Mishka need to talk to him away from everyone? This walk of punishment had pain written all over it. Mishka had said he'd discipline him if he didn't obey him. The problem

191

was Ben hadn't thought for one minute that he was doing anything wrong when he decided to go with Kylan. After all, Ben owed his life to Kylan. His father never cared where he went as long as Kylan was with him. However, Mishka didn't feel the same way about Kylan as his father had. Mishka saw him as a threat.

When Mishka opened the door at the end of the hallway, Ben gasped. It was one of those BDSM playrooms. The dungeon furniture included a swing, spanking horses, a vertical bondage rack, a large cage, and a spanking bench. On one of the walls, floggers, whips, crops, paddles, and canes hung on hooks. The bookshelves included wrist and ankle shackles in leather and steel, spreader bars, blindfolds, and gags. Another shelf held nipples clamps of varying intensity, leather hoods, violet wands, chastity devices, and leather restraints.

"Do you know why I brought you in here?" Mishka asked.

"I doubt it's to do a scene with me." Ben scanned the room as he inhaled the fresh leather smell. Everything in the room appeared brand new and unused.

"Do you know why I'm furious with you?" Mishka asked.

"Because I refused to betray Kylan."

"That's right. Do you remember I asked for your loyalty and respect as my lover?"

"Yes, I remember." Ben's sight hung on the huge dog cage in the corner. There was no way he'd ever go in there. Inside the cage was a green padded mat. It looked brand new and unused.

"You broke your promise to me. Don't ever disrespect me again."

"I'm sorry, but you put me in a no win situation. I owe Kylan my life."

"I promised I'd hire Kylan to guard you, and I'll keep that promise. I warned you if you break my rules, I'll punish you. And you agreed to it."

"I don't know what to say other than I'm sorry I disrespected you." Ben lowered his eyes with the hope that Mishka would see how sorry he was.

"If you don't want me to punish you, then you're choosing not to be my lover. I'll still protect you, but we won't be anything to each other and you'll sleep in your own room."

Ben thought about what Mishka had said. He could walk out of here as a free man and escape his punishment, or he could accept the punishment and Mishka would continue to work on a relationship between them. He didn't

193

much like his choices and right now, he had no idea where he'd go if he left. He had no one on his side except Mishka and Kylan.

"I'll take my punishment." Ben hoped he wouldn't regret his decision. The truth was he wanted to stay with Mishka, or at least he thought he did. He should have told him the truth and not lied to him, but how could he betray Kylan? He felt trapped in this room and needed some space outside.

"Stand by the spanking bench." Mishka pointed to it.

Ben moved to the other side of the room and waited. Mishka was going to whip him until he hurt. There was no getting out of it now unless he wanted to throw their relationship out the door. He'd have to get smarter about making sure Mishka never caught him breaking a rule.

Mishka unzipped Ben's jeans and roughly pulled them and his underwear down.

"Step out of them before you trip."

Ben was sporting a hard on, and this wasn't the right time for that. How could his dick find enjoyment of some unknown punishment for being disrespectful? He thrived on pain. But he didn't like the disappointment in Mishka's face.

"Bend over."

194

Ben slowly leaned over the leather-spanking bench. Mishka handcuffed his hands and feet to the bench. With all Mishka's talk about not being his sub, he sure felt like one at the moment.

The loud sound of Mishka's belt sliding through the loops of his pants made Ben clench his ass cheeks.

"I'm punishing you for lying to me and disrespecting me." Mishka's voice was void of emotion, a distancing Ben feared.

Ben nodded, unable to speak. He heard the snapping sound of the belt as Mishka sailed it through the air behind him. When the thick belt landed on his ass cheeks, Ben bit his lower lip to keep from making any noise. Mishka wasted no time whipping his ass with the belt. It felt like he was swinging the belt as hard as he could. Ben arched his back, hoping to derail part of the sting.

He's never going to stop.

Ben never had a chance to catch his breath—Mishka's belt pounded him continually for what seemed to be a long time. He cried silently from the shame and pain. The belt lit a fire on his ass. He had never known this much anguish and humiliation from a punishment. There was no doubt in his mind that he'd obey Mishka's orders from now on. His panic slowly turned to hate and anger. Could he love a man who beat him for being disrespectful? He doubted his feelings at the moment. Maybe he should inform Kylan he wanted to leave and hide out somewhere else. The whipping messed up his emotions and he was totally unprepared for it, though Mishka had warned him. He obviously didn't heed his words.

"Get dressed."

Mishka watched him dress and handed him a bottle of water.

"Drink this."

"Thank you," Ben said, then drank the water.

"I want you, Ben, but I can't accept dishonesty and disrespect. Do you think you can work on that?"

"Yes, Sir."

Mishka put his arms around Ben and kissed him. "You don't know how much I want you to be mine."

"I want to be with you, but there has to be some boundaries when it comes to Kylan. He has been with me for four years. He saved my life and we're friends. I don't see him as a lover. He's like a big brother to me."

Mishka checked his watch. "It's seven o'clock, so dinner is ready." Mishka didn't respond to Ben's comments and took his hand leading him to the dining room.

196

The dinner table had nametags on their plates. Mishka had assigned Ben to the head of the table at the end opposite Mishka. Miss Daria and Kylan sat across from each other.

Miss Daria passed the plates to Mishka first, then it went around to the others. Ben thought the table was so long he might need to shout to be heard. His ass was sore, but the padded chair was better than a wooden one.

"I want to inform all of you that Ben isn't to leave this house without my permission. My point is to keep him safe. Once this mess is settled, Ben is free to go where he wants. I plan to discuss the situation with my father again. I'd like to speed up the process."

Ben looked over at Kylan and smiled.

"Ben's safety is the most important thing right now," Kylan said.

"I also don't want any visitors inside my home unless you clear it with me first," Mishka said.

"I'm starting to feel like a prisoner," Ben said.

"You're not a prisoner. You're my beautiful lover and I cherish you. That's why I want you to stay home until things are safe."

"There are tons of things here to do," Miss Daria said. "The swimming pool is the best. We have an exercise room too."

"I need my laptops," Ben said. "My two laptops are at my condos."

"Jasha could get them for you," Mishka said.

"I could take a run to your New York condo and get that one with some more things you might need," Kylan said.

"That's a great idea," Mishka said. "I don't want Ben unhappy while I'm working."

After a quiet dinner, Mishka told Ben to wait for him by the pool and to enjoy a bottle of wine until he returned from his meeting with Kylan. Miss Daria stayed in the kitchen cleaning up and avoided Ben for some reason. It would have been nice if she would join him outside, so he would have someone to talk to. Ben wondered how much she knew about Mishka. Did she ever see the other wing of the house? It was clean so either she was in there to clean or Mishka could have locked her out of there and had one of his subs clean it or maybe he cleaned that wing himself.

BRINA BRADY

CHAPTER NINETEEN

Mishka

Mishka sat down behind his desk when Kylan entered and sat on the chair opposite.

"Look, I know you're upset with Ben and me. I told you Ben fights for what he wants. It isn't going to be easy for him to follow every order you bark at him. You might want to talk to him with a softer tone and explain why."

"Is that how you relate to him?" Mishka asked.

"I speak to Ben with respect as he does to me. His family tends to shout at him, and he doesn't like it one bit. I'm just trying to give you some insight into Ben's ways."

"What did your source say?"

"When we were at the Chinese restaurant, he sent me a text and told me that Sal put a hit on us. So I told Ben we had to leave for security reasons. I also saw some of Sal's men at the restaurant which made me think it was true. I opened Sal's envelope. Inside was a check for one hundred thousand dollars. He thanked me for saving Ben's life, which made me think he didn't order the hit. Why would he thank me and hand over so much money?"

"I hate Sal. I don't trust him and prefer not to work with him or his family on anything. I don't know why he would give you so much money if he put a hit on both of you. But it doesn't make sense."

"So today, I found out it was Dante. We don't get along with him. Sal hired Dante and me to guard Ben at night when he was cruising around. But my source said Dante wasn't alone. He had help from one of Ben's brothers. This is why I didn't want to say anything in front of him. He didn't know which brother. Sal will never believe that. His allegiance is to his sons and Dante," Kylan said.

"So, we either begin a war with the Banetti's by taking out Dante and one of the brothers, or they take out Ben. I don't like this at all. I'll discuss this with my father. This is a very delicate matter. Ben doesn't need to know about one of his brothers helping Dante. But I do think Ben knows Dante was in on it," Mishka said.

"Yes, Ben knew Dante had something to do with it, but he wouldn't say anything because he doesn't want to start a war with his family," Kylan said.

"I think someone should take out Dante first. They both have to go. I'm not sure how to deal with this without starting a war with them. My father knows how to get things done without a war. He knows how to deal with Sal too. Are there any factions within the Banetti family who want to take over Sal's family?"

"That I don't know. Nico would know."

"Do you know Nico well?"

"Yes. I could talk to him without Sal finding out. I've talked to him in private before. He's very protective of Ben, and he knows how to talk to Sal."

"I'm going to talk to my father first, then I'll get back to you if I need you to talk to Nico."

"Is that all?" Kylan asked.

"Yes. Are you going somewhere?"

"Jasha is coming over and we're going to play pool."

"Jasha? Oh, I didn't know he was coming over."

"He said he's staying over for the weekend."

"That's good."

Mishka wanted to talk to Ben to make sure he was okay after his punishment. He could see why he was so loyal to Kylan because that man definitely had his back. He didn't have his family anymore. Kylan was the one he depended on and he always came through for him. He found Ben drinking wine on the lounge chair.

"I finished talking to Kylan."

"What did he say?"

"He didn't mention his gun going off, but I suppose he didn't want to brag about killing someone. He thinks Dante is the one who put a hit on you." Mishka didn't want Ben to know about one of his brothers helping Dante.

"Dante couldn't do that alone. He's not that organized, and he doesn't have enough money to pay for a hit," Ben said.

"I don't know Dante at all except from his immature behavior at the luncheon."

"We have a long history—a bad history—together. I believe he wants me gone, and he hates Kylan. But he just doesn't have it in him to do that on his own."

"I'm going to talk to my father tonight to see how to deal with this. But right now, I want to make sure we're okay."

"You mean after you beat me?"

"Yes. I warned you about my rules."

"The problem is I didn't see what I did as breaking a rule. You did say to stay home, but leaving with my security guard shouldn't be a security issue."

"So you believe you were wrongly punished?"

"Literally, no, but in the spirit of my action, yes."

"Don't talk circles around me. It's a yes or no answer."

"Then my answer is no."

203

"So you want new rules concerning Kylan?"

"If you think I'll be safer here than leaving, I'll stay here. I had to help Kylan, especially after what he did for me."

"That's a step in the right direction. I do understand how you feel, but it doesn't affect my reason to discipline you for breaking my rules. I'm not allowing some asshole to take you out for whatever reason. If you need to go to Columbia University, I trust Kylan to go with you. He needs to heal properly first though. I also hear your reservations about Dante. So do you think he had a partner?"

"My grandfather left me the Banetti Ristorante and some property in Florida. My brother Freddie thought my grandfather should have given it to him. The thing is Freddie never gave my grandfather or grandmother the time of day. I spent weekends with them when I was growing up. I wanted to go there; Freddie never wanted to visit them."

"So what are you saying?"

"If I have an enemy beside Dante, it would be Freddie. He hates me, and so does Carmen for that matter. My father had planned to divide his property and money between all three of us. Now that he has disowned me, they can divide it between the two of them."

"I don't see any reason why your brothers would help Dante. Your father disowned you, so they got what they wanted without you dead."

"I wasn't disowned when the shots were fired."

"True."

"Are you still angry with me?"

"I never was angry. I just thought you needed to learn a lesson if you want to be with me."

"I still don't see the difference between you whipping me for disrespecting you and a sub being disciplined by his Dom. The only difference is you didn't allow me to safeword out."

"You can't safeword out of discipline for bad behavior."

"Then you haven't read any books on BDSM."

"Now you're insulting me? Are you saying I never read a book?"

"Any action between a Dom and sub must have an exit," Ben said.

"Did you study BDSM at Columbia?" Mishka asked.

"No. Doms make the rules, but the sub must agree."

"You're not my sub. Got you."

"Still, if you want to protect me, we should come to an agreement."

"Wow! You're bold to talk to me like that."

"You know, Mishka, I like you a lot and want us to work, but you seem to think I have no say or choice in the matter around here. I appreciate you helping Kylan and me. I just think we need to do more negotiations."

"I need to call my father. Write a list of things you want to negotiate with me. We'll discuss it when I finish talking to him. If you ever have ambitions of becoming my sub, you're going to have to take a back seat in decision-making though. Maybe you need to read up on submission."

"Yes, Sir." Ben poured himself more wine.

"Don't get too drunk."

"No, Sir."

Mishka made his way to his office thinking that Ben was a piece of work and needed some taming. How the hell did he get so damn bold? Yes, he was a brat who needed a few whippings to put him in his place. After he closed his door, he cleared Ben from his mind, and called his father.

"What's up, Mishka? More problems?"

"Kylan found out more information on the shooters and who might have ordered it."

"Really. What did he say?"

"He said Dante Banetti ordered the hit but he had financial assistance from one of Ben's brothers. He didn't know which one. We didn't tell Ben about one of his brothers being part of it. I told Ben it was Dante, but he didn't think Dante could do it alone. He also mentioned his older brother Freddie was angry at Ben because their grandfather left the Banetti Ristorante to only Ben."

"That's some pretty heavy shit going on in that family. We could take out Dante to send a message, but I'm not sure either of those brothers would stop. I really hate to think Sal had encouraged his sons to do this heinous crime against his own son."

"Sal disowned Ben so he won't get anything. What would be the reason then?" Mishka asked.

"I don't know, but those two boys are stupid and evil. Sal never discussed Ben ever. I found out about Ben when your mother went to visit Ben's mother in Florida."

"Yes, she loved going to Florida with her sisters and cousins. They had a great time."

"She sure did. I miss her more than you'll ever know."

"I know you do. I feel the same way."

"I'm going to think on what you told me before I find a solution. Meanwhile, keep both of them home."

207

"I can't control Kylan, and I hope Ben will listen."

"Make him listen even if you have to chain him in his room. His life depends on it."

"Maybe I should stay home and let Jasha take care of things."

"That's a good idea. Thank God, we have Jasha."

CHAPTER TWENTY

Ben

Ben took a shower after he had a swim in the pool, then he sat on the bed and looked up submission on a BDSM site. Mishka turned him on, but after the sex was done, he wasn't sure he liked him bossing him around so much. His jealousy was out of the box to a point of Ben being uncomfortable with his behavior. He threw his coffee mug against the wall over Kylan. There were some stop signs signaling he may not be safe for Ben. One thing Ben had learned was to defend himself against any abuse. Mishka had no right to tell him what he can or can't do with Kylan. He didn't want to make a big deal about him since Mishka was so damn jealous of him. What was he doing with another mob boss? He was with a man who did things Ben objected to, but had he gotten so used to living like this that he didn't see the problems lurking in front of him. Mishka dangled the Dom and sub thing to get him to accept things he didn't want to. That was where negotiation came in.

Ben's phone buzzed with a message, and he had no idea who it was.

Unknown: *You're going to die soon. You'll end up with cement tied around your ankles in the ocean.*

Ben hadn't given his number out to anyone. Kylan and Mishka were the only ones with it. He certainly wasn't going to answer it. Was Mishka testing him with the message to see if he would tell him? At this point, he worried Mishka had turned against him. Maybe Kylan did too. He walked to Kylan's bedroom and knocked on the door.

"Come in," Kylan said. "What's the matter?"

"I'm fucked up. Mishka went all Dom on me, then he tells me that he isn't my Dom. But he is dictating to me as if I were his sub. And I'm afraid he will come between you and me."

"Sit down. We'll talk." Kylan padded the side of his bed.

Ben studied Kylan's expression and immediately felt safe and calmer. He still had Kylan on his side so he sat down.

"Here's what I think. You need a strong Dom and don't get mad, but you're on the bratty side. You want to control everything, but your needs betray you. I wished you'd met a professor at college and would have gotten out of this world, but you met Mishka. He truly cares for you. I

211

don't think you'll find a guy who will love how you challenge him and care for you in such a short time. His father seems to approve of you too. Give him a chance. Don't worry about me. I'll always be in your life. No one will come between us. You're the little brother I never had. If he ever hurts you, tell me. That's my advice, Ben."

"You think he cares for me?"

"Yes. And as far as him going all Dom on you, this just tells me he wants you as his sub so badly, but he won't do it until he has your complete trust. He's right about that. Don't fight him. Try to understand him and remember I'm always here for you."

"Thanks, Kylan. Too bad you weren't around when I was growing up."

"But I'm here now. Where's Mishka?"

"He's on the phone with his father."

Kylan checked his phone. "I've got to go downstairs. Jasha is here."

"Are you and Jasha a thing?"

"I think Jasha is confused. I'm not sure what he wants. We're just getting to know each other. You know… just talking."

"Interesting. Have fun." Ben hugged Kylan, then left.

He found Mishka in the bed reading his tablet. He looked up at Ben. "Where were you?"

"Talking to Kylan."

"I see. I spoke to my father and he said he wants to investigate a peaceful solution with your family. But quite frankly, I don't see a path of non-violence."

"I don't know what I should do anymore."

"Ben, try to trust me to do right by you."

"Are we going to talk about negotiations between us?"

"I'd rather fuck you, instead. But I promised we would."

"For us to work on any level, you have to understand I have a relationship with Kylan. As I said, he's like an older brother. I don't want to be torn between you and him. I want both of you in my life, but you can't go off when something doesn't suit you, and make me betray him. He would never do that when it comes to you."

"That's a reasonable demand. I can agree to that. But if it comes to breaking my rules and doing something with Kylan, you need to talk to me first. There will always be consequences to rule breaking."

"Right now, you said I have to respect you and stay loyal. I can do that."

"Okay, see that you do."

"Yes, Sir."

"I'm staying home tomorrow. My father will probably visit us."

"I need to show you something."

"Then show me instead of talking about it."

Ben handed his phone to Mishka.

"Who the hell knows your new phone number? Did you give it out to anyone?"

"No. Only you and Kylan. No one else."

"The driver got the phone. Either we were followed or the driver sold your number. Did you show this to Kylan?"

"No, I thought I'd show you first," Ben lied. He'd meant to show it to Kylan but had totally forgotten because he was too upset with Mishka.

"I'm going to forward this to my father."

"Did I do something wrong?" Ben asked, worried Mishka would become angry at him all over again.

"No, Ben. Let's go and show Kylan as well."

"He's with Jasha."

"We'll show him later then. Do you think that's odd that they're spending so much time together?" Mishka asked.

"I don't know. I guess they like to talk to each other."

"Ben, let's go to bed. My father just returned my text and said he'll be over in the morning."

Ben undressed and climbed under the covers with Mishka.

"Ben, I don't want us to fight anymore."

"I don't want to fight with you, either."

Sudden movement in the bed confused Ben. Mishka hugged him and pushed his tongue into his mouth with such passion. Ben responded by sucking and biting. Their tongues tugged against each other as Mishka's hands wandered all over Ben's body. He pulled away from Ben, staring at him with pride.

"Get on your side," Mishka whispered as he rested on his side.

Ben turned on his side facing Mishka, who reached for the lube and a condom sitting on the nightstand. He put on and lubed the condom and the outside area of Ben's opening. He was rock hard against Mishka's erection. He entered Ben with one finger, stretching him. Ben moaned when the second finger moved in. He arched to take more, but Mishka pulled his fingers out and replaced them with his cockhead. He moved it in deeper, more urgently, further burning him. Mishka grabbed his nipples, twisting them until Ben jerked from pain and pleasure.

"I love your nip rings."

"I love when you play with them." Ben stiffened.

Mishka pounded his hole, which ignited in him an urgency to come. Hitting Ben's prostate made him shudder throughout. Ben was rocking in time with him, allowing him to hammer his cock in the deepest possible way.

"Make yourself come," Mishka ordered as he handed the lube bottle to him.

Ben lubed his cock and his hand, then stroked it while Mishka pounded his hole.

"Ahh. Feels so good," Ben panted.

"Take it," Mishka moaned.

Mishka shot his cum inside his condom, causing Ben to spurt his.

"Fuck. Fuck. Fuck," Mishka shouted and then collapsed beside Ben.

"Ahhh. Ahhh," Ben moaned.

Ben sat up when Mishka left the room to get them some bottled water to drink. When he returned, he had made popcorn. He set the tray on Ben's lap until he got into the bed.

"I thought we could watch a movie," Mishka said.

"Sounds like a good idea to me." Ben kissed Mishka.

CHAPTER TWENTY-ONE

Mishka

The next day, they met his father for breakfast. He wasn't sure Ben trusted him enough to share his feelings about last night. Yes, they fucked under the sheets, but what was Ben thinking? Was he here only for protection or did he want to be here? Only time would tell and Mishka wasn't a patient man.

Miss Daria served them hot coffee on the patio overlooking the pool while they waited for his father. Kylan and Jasha joined them at the table. He didn't know what to make about the two of them. They had private conversations as if they were lovers, but that didn't make any sense. Jasha had never declared he was gay. Why wouldn't he if he was? There would be no reason to hide his preference for men. Or was Kylan taking advantage of Jasha? He was a lonely soul who never had any sex as far as Mishka had known and he certainly never discussed it.

"What are you two planning today?" Mishka asked Jasha and Kylan.

"We're going to pick up Ben's laptop in New Jersey and pack up some of his summer clothes," Kylan said.

"My father will be here soon, so could you wait for him. He may have some questions, Kylan," Mishka asked.

"Sure. No problem."

Within a few minutes, Mishka's father joined them at the table. Mishka moved and let his father sit at the head.

"Morning!" Shurik said.

They all exchanged pleasantries while Miss Daria poured more coffee for all of them, then she sat down at the table with them.

"Have you spoken to my father?" Ben asked.

"No. I'm not going to go through him until I get more information on your cousin Dante."

"Sir, it's not just him," Ben said.

"Ben, I'm sorry you're going through this. No one wants to have their freedom cut because some asshole is selfish and evil. Can you make me a promise that you'll stay here until we find a solution? Nothing will be done without your consent," Shurik said.

"Yes, sir. I'm not moving from the house."

"That will keep my blood pressure lower if you do. Mishka can't protect you if you're out and about without him. As soon as Kylan heals, he'll be able to secure your safety," Shurik said.

219

Once they were finished eating, Miss Daria refilled their coffee cups again. She cleared the table and remained in the kitchen.

"Here's the deal, if Dante is responsible, then we can put a hit on him. That's my last resort. Kylan, could you have a meeting with Nico and feel him out? I'll have you covered with security," Shurik said.

"Yes, sir. He has Ben's interest at heart. By now, he's probably sniffing around to find the shooters too," Kylan said.

"I checked on the driver who purchased the phone for Ben. You had hired him last month, Mishka. I fired him this morning, and there will be another driver from one of our trusted families. I also spoke to the store manager, and he told me he fired the salesman because one of the other employees said he had taken money for the phone number," Shurik said.

"You did all that this morning?" Mishka had gotten this guy from Miss Daria who suggested him. That will be the last time he takes any suggestion from her. Did someone befriend her to get at Ben and Kylan? That he didn't know, but would like to find out.

"No. I worked on some of it last night. Be careful who you hire."

220

"I will," Mishka said. His brain must have short-circuited when he accepted her suggestion, but he had interviewed him, and there wasn't any sign he was there for information.

"Thanks for the breakfast. And, Ben, stay home and out of trouble."

They all stood to say their goodbyes to Shurik. Soon after, Jasha and Kylan left for the New Jersey shore. Mishka and Ben were at the table alone.

"So, what are we going to do all day?" Ben asked.

"We're going to get to know each other all over again. How about that?" Mishka asked.

"As in you didn't like how we met?"

"I wish I had known more about you when I fucked you in the alley. We could have gone on a proper date, but we didn't."

"You got into my head. I wanted more and you gave so little. Then I found out who you were, I thought you were an impossibility. It didn't stop me from wanting to see you. I only stopped when I knew who you were."

"I don't regret taking you into my world. I know you wanted to get away from this because that is what I wanted too. But you see how good my father is to me. I could never say no to him for anything, so I took over for him out

221

of respect. I couldn't walk away, not after all he has done for me. But you did what I wanted to do."

"Now that you're in charge you can make the changes you want to see happen."

"Ben, I have tried to go legitimate, but everyone, including my father, has fought me. My father told me to make the business what it should be. Yet, you saw how he caved to your father. I still have your Banetti family running drugs and whores in my clubs. That's the last thing I wanted."

"That's not really true. Your father made a deal to keep us safe. It's all about negotiations during the deal. I fear my father will break the deal with yours."

"Are you back to thinking your father put a hit on you?" Mishka asked. He could see it in Ben's eyes that he believed his family wanted him dead. What a horrible way to feel about your family. He held Ben's hand, lifting it up to his lips, and kissed it.

"I don't know what I believe."

"No harm will come to you, but I can't erase the pain of your family plotting against you. I can offer you the love from my family and me. I know you're hurting, and it must feel like you're all alone. Remember you have my family and me plus you have Kylan as a great friend."

"Thank you. I'll feel better when I get back to work and on a case study. I wanted to join one in August. That's why I wanted my laptop, so I can apply. I also wanted to help at the shelter, and now I can't. I won't put the boys at risk because of me."

"Let's hope we can solve this problem without spilling more blood," Mishka said.

"I doubt it can be solved without violence of some kind."

"Want to help build something with me?" Mishka saw Ben going darker in his mood and needed something to move his thoughts to something else.

"Sure. What are we going to build?" Ben asked.

"Come and I'll show you."

They walked to the other end of the house and down the stairs to the basement.

"I'm making a St. Andrews Cross," Mishka said and pointed to the unfinished wood.

"Your playroom looks brand new. Did you make some of the furniture?" Ben asked.

"I did. Everything is new in there. I started working on it two years ago. I hate to admit this, but no one has ever been in that room except you. I wanted a playroom with part of me in the creation. But I never could find anyone to

223

play in there. Well, none that I trusted. Now, you're here. We'll see how things work out between us."

"It's awesome. It looks like a private BDSM club."

"Thank you. I did everything myself." Mishka opened two cans of stain and handed Ben a brush.

"Do you know how to stain?" Mishka asked.

"I've done it before."

They sat on the floor beside each other staining the wood panels. Later, they cleaned up and set the wood to dry.

"Excellent job, Ben."

"Thank you. That was fun working with you. I usually do everything alone."

"I know you said you had taken a trip alone to Europe. Would you go to Russia with me?"

"I've always wanted to visit, but my father never allowed it. He took me to Europe and of course, many times to Italy. The Banetti's have relatives there."

"If I can see my way through a couple of things, would you travel to Russia with me?" Mishka asked Ben again since he didn't find his answer in his reply.

"It sounds like a lot of fun."

"So is that a yes, or a no?" Mishka asked yet another time to find out his answer. For some reason, Ben didn't

224

respond to him directly. He always circled around words without committing to an answer. No one could accuse Ben of being too direct.

"It's a happy yes in all caps."

"Let's go to the bedroom and play."

"Can we play in the playroom?"

"You're getting wild, Ben. After last night, I thought you'd never want to return to that room."

"But you're not angry at me anymore."

Mishka's hands touched his cheek, moving down to his chin. He lifted Ben's chin to kiss him. "You're so much prettier up close. My sweet Ben."

CHAPTER TWENTY-TWO

Ben

They entered the playroom, which once again smelled of new leather. Mishka drew the darkened drapes across the window and locked the door.

"Remove your clothes and kneel in the center with your head lowered," Mishka ordered.

Mishka kept his eyes fixed on Ben's form the entire time. He pried off his shoes and socks. He removed his T-shirt and carefully hung it over the back of the chair. Then he pulled down his jeans and folded them neatly. When Ben dropped his jockstrap, Mishka kissed him, punctuating his nakedness.

Ben's body became putty in Mishka's hands. He knew all his special spots, especially that one inside of him. He might be rough with Ben's body at times, but he always knew how to make him come in the end. Ben's gasps and moans often ignited a flame in him that Ben didn't know existed. He definitely didn't behave like the same man in the alley and he no longer just fucked Ben before leaving him alone in a dirty alley.

"Since you requested to play in here, would you like me to use some bondage items?"

"What did you have in mind, Sir?" Ben liked calling him Sir, in this room in particular. It made him feel like he was his real sub, even when Mishka made sure to inform Ben he wasn't. But here he was in a BDSM playroom with Mishka pretending he was.

"Every time you call me Sir, my cock grows bigger. Pick out the things you want me to use on you. No spanking implements tonight. You need to heal my sweet Benjie." He handed Ben a basket for the items.

"What are those metal things on shelf two used for?"

"The long one is called a spreader to force your legs apart. The other is the wand. It shocks you."

Ben walked over to the shelf, picking up various handcuffs, putting the green furry ones into the basket. He chose a matching satin blindfold and a green feather. He checked out all the vibrating butt plugs, added one to the basket, and returned them to Mishka.

"Good choices, Ben."

Ben was excited to share an experience with Mishka in his playroom. He had chosen safe items, nothing he hadn't used before.

227

Mishka tied the blindfold around Ben's eyes. "Can you see?"

"No, Sir."

"Is it too tight?" Mishka ran his hand down Ben's back in a loving way.

"No, Sir. It fits fine."

"Now, since we're playing with a few bondage items, use the traffic light colors. Red to stop, yellow to pause, and green to continue."

Ben had read about traffic light code for notifying the Dom of the sub's physical and emotional state during a scene. He sure felt like a sub in this room with Mishka. He said he wanted Ben to trust him before they could have a BDSM relationship. One thing about Mishka, he was a man who was super sensitive with trust and respect issues. Someday, Mishka might give reasons for Ben to trust him, but it will take time. And Mishka was right, Ben felt safe because Kylan was around him.

"Lie face-down on the table and spread your legs and arms." Mishka helped him to the padded table. He tied Ben's ankles to the table legs and then cuffed his wrists to the hooks above it. "You're so damn hot, boy." Mishka used the green feather, running the feather up and down Ben's body, tickling him.

228

"That tickles me in a good way," Ben said.

"I'm going to feather torture you to prepare you." He continued outlining his back, buttocks, and legs with the feather.

Ben sucked in a breath and arched into the touch while Mishka tickled him with the feather. Ben's laughing overtook him; his erection was underneath him smacking his stomach. He didn't know why but his cock stretched further. *Fuck, he's going to make him come from tickling.*

After feathering Ben, Mishka rubbed lube around his opening. He slipped the vibrating plug inside. "How does it feel?"

"It feels big."

"Too big?"

"It'll feel better if it vibrates," Ben said. "I'm not telling you what to do, just suggesting, Sir."

Mishka turned the power to slow, and it buzzed softly, then when he hiked up the power, his ass was buzzing. "Do you like it now?"

"Hmm." Ben enjoyed it so much he couldn't speak words. The pressure and vibrating on his prostate enhanced his pleasure.

Mishka rubbed his back while the vibrating butt plug buzzed.

229

"Please fuck me, Sir?"

"If your ass wasn't red still, I'd paddle you." Mishka turned off the power and removed it from Ben's ass. He felt empty right away.

"You would?"

"Learn your place in my playroom."

"Yes, Sir."

Mishka unzipped his jeans, put on a condom with lube, then he pushed his cock all the way inside Ben in one long stroke. He felt the whole length of his cock all the way along his tunnel; the walls inside tingled and burned at once. He loved the feeling of warmth and hardness, the motion of Mishka's steel cock moving back and forth. Then Mishka's tempo moved faster and harder as he pumped. Mishka's huge cock was fucking him; the only care Ben wanted at the moment. Mishka's balls were warm and silk soft when their bodies touched.

"Push your ass out further boy." Mishka smacked Ben's ass.

Ben lifted his ass up and Mishka placed a pillow under his stomach.

"That's it, I'm going to bang the cum out of you."

Ben moved to the rhythm of his thrust.

"Do it, Sir," Ben said, pushing his ass up and back the best he could for Mishka.

"I love that. Keep pushing back to meet me. You horny boy. You want my big dick, don't you? Give it up, boy; give your ass to me. Push back harder, boy," Mishka said.

Mishka's fisted Ben's cock, milking him until he was ready to shoot. He wanted to wait for Mishka's order. His heavy breathing and faster thrust told him Mishka would be ready soon.

Mishka panted, "Fuck. You're a good fuck." He came inside his condom. "Come with me."

Ben shot warm cum into Mishka's hand. He wiped it on Ben's ass while they panted in their sweat. Mishka removed the handcuffs and the straps on his ankles after he pulled out of him. He wiped Ben's ass and cock. He flipped him on his back and removed the blindfold.

"I love that you wanted to try some bondage with me," Mishka said, planting warm kisses all over his face. He moved his tongue inside Ben's mouth. Their tongues battled with passion.

"I trust you to make me come," Ben said, overjoyed Mishka was pleased with him. They ventured into the bathroom for a shower. They spent the rest of the time watching a movie in bed.

231

***

The next day, Ben rolled over in bed beside Mishka who was asleep. He had been working nonstop lately, trying to keep Ben safe from the threats. Hiding out in his own home took its toll on him. Yet, he was the only one who could order a hit on Dante, but he didn't. Much of their alone time was interrupted by phone calls. Ben didn't want to disturb Mishka from his much-needed rest with a morning blowjob, so he feather-kissed the back of his neck. Ben slipped out of bed, stopped at the bathroom, and tiptoed to the kitchen. He turned on the old coffee machine, looking through the window into the morning darkness. A tall man exited from the guesthouse, surrounded by the thickness of many trees. There was something familiar about the man, but he couldn't pinpoint it. He could have sworn the guy looked like that new driver who sold his phone number. The man was the same height and weight as the fired driver. She couldn't be seeing him after Mishka's father had fired him. Why would she see him or worse, why would he be seeing her? Maybe he was seeing things that weren't there. He wouldn't mention this to anyone since he wasn't sure, and he didn't want to get Miss Daria in trouble with Mishka.

232

He paced on the wooden floor until the coffee dripped to fill his mug, and he made one for Mishka. Both of them drank their coffee black which made it easy.

When Ben carried the coffee on a tray to the bedroom, Mishka was sitting up in bed and shouting to someone on the phone right before he ended the call. Carefully, Ben handed him a tall mug of steaming coffee. The way Mishka had been shouting on the phone reminded him how his father dealt with his employees. It wasn't a side Ben had admired of his father or did of Mishka. Ben preferred dealing with facts with seriousness and without strong emotions such as shouting.

"Thank you, Ben. That was so sweet of you to bring me coffee in bed."

Ben sat beside Mishka on the bed with his coffee. "Is everything okay?"

"Ben, I can't discuss business with you."

"Is that because I'm a Banetti or you don't trust me?" Ben asked.

"Maybe a little of both when it comes to business. But I want that to change at some point in our relationship."

CHAPTER TWENTY-THREE

Mishka

All morning they swam laps in the pool and played games. After drying off, Mishka and Ben relaxed on lounges by the pool, and Miss Daria served them each a Pina Colada. She told them she had some errands to attend to and would return in a few hours. She did all the grocery shopping for the house and dropped off Mishka's suits and shirts to the dry cleaners.

"I heard from Kylan and they will be staying at your place overnight because it was taking longer than they had thought to pack up," Mishka said, wondering what those two were up to in Ben's condo. He wondered if Ben wanted to move out, or did he want to hold onto it?

"Really? I didn't ask them to pack up everything," Ben said,

"Maybe they wanted to spend some time alone," Mishka said.

"That might be. It's really nice at my condo. I love living there."

"I wouldn't mind staying there from time to time."

234

"If we could figure out how to stop someone from trying to kill me, we could spend some time there," Ben said.

"Ben, we're going to figure this out. Try not to think about it."

"It's difficult for me to believe Dante hated me enough that he'd have me killed."

"You and I were both born in families that don't value life. Some see it a means to an end."

The front door opened and his father walked into the living room. Mishka and Ben stood. Shurik kissed Mishka on each cheek, which Mishka returned, then he wrapped Ben in his powerful arms and greeted him in the same manner.

"Sit down. I have some bad news." A small frown swept across his father's face. The circles beneath his eyes darkened from overworking in the evenings. He looked like he hadn't slept many hours.

Mishka and Ben sat down beside each other on the couch and waited with apprehension.

"What's wrong?" Ben asked.

"Jasha was shot on the beach in New Jersey. Apparently, he had decided to take a walk alone on the beach while Kylan was packing your things. He's in the hospital recovering with Kylan at his side," his father said.

"Is it really bad?" Ben asked.

"He'll be getting out tomorrow. I have a limo picking them both up with Ben's things."

"What happened? Whoever the fuck did this must pay," Mishka shouted.

"No one knows yet. I haven't talked to Jasha because he was in surgery. Kylan thinks it's the same people, but we don't operate on hearsay. We need the facts."

"It's my fault this happened. I should leave your home because I'm causing too many problems for your family," Ben said.

"Stop talking like that, Ben. You're not going anywhere." Mishka's forehead brushed against Ben's and he found himself lost in his blue eyes.

"Ben, you didn't make them do this. And no, it's not your fault you're a Banetti either. I want all four of you out of the country. I'm making plans to fly you all to Russia," Shurik said.

"How will that solve anything?" Mishka asked.

"Mishka, you and Jasha can't do business when someone is plotting to end both of you. If they went after

Jasha and Ben, you're next. We have to get to the root of this problem."

"What does that even mean?" Ben asked.

"It means if your family was responsible, then there will be bloodshed. I'm sorry," Shurik said.

"If the Banetti family did this to Jasha, I don't want them selling drugs in my clubs. I'll call the fucking cops on them," Mishka said.

"You mean on my uncle Tony?" Ben asked.

"For someone who isn't working for the family, you sure know a lot," Mishka said.

"I'm not stupid. I listen to what goes on around me," Ben said.

"We must cut all ties with Sal and his family. I set up a virtual meeting with Sal," his father said.

"When?" Mishka asked.

"Now," Shurik said.

Mishka led them down the long hallway to the large room with ten laptops and all sorts of other electronic devices. He used it for his men plotting and investigating. There was a whiteboard at the front for Mishka when he instructed his men.

"Don't turn on the camera, Ben. I don't want your father to see you," his father said.

Ben sat three seats away from Mishka when both of them joined the online room. Sal was already waiting with Nico.

"What's this meeting about?" Sal asked with a grumpy voice.

"Jasha was shot yesterday in Wildwood. What's going on?" Shurik asked.

"Should I know about this?" Sal asked.

"We did some investigating and found out who put a hit on Kylan and Ben. We believe the same people shot my son Jasha," Shurik said.

"And who did this?"

"Dante and one of your sons," Shurik said.

"That's bullshit. My sons and Dante would never put a hit on Ben or anyone else without my order. Every order comes from me."

"You can do what you want with this information. We're cutting all ties with your family as of today. Expect retaliation," Shurik said.

"That means get your men out of my clubs," Mishka said.

Within a minute, Sal's profile blacked out and he left the online room.

"Now what?" Ben asked.

"Unfortunately, we might have to take Dante down at some point. We don't know which brother is involved, so we'll wait to find out more facts," Shurik said.

"I don't know what to say." Ben stared with wide-open eyes, like the whole world was crumbling apart around him… he didn't shake… just froze in total paralysis realizing how much he had been hated.

"No one is safe with Dante around. Your father will probably check it out first, and then we'll see what he does, so we won't act on it immediately. He won't like losing business so he's motivated to find the shooters," Shurik said.

"He says a lot of things, but after he thinks and researches things, he'll change his mind if it benefits him in some way," Ben said.

"Ben, I want you safe as much as I want my sons safe. This is why all four of you are going to stay in Russia away from here. I'll come over tomorrow when Jasha and Kylan return. That's when I'll give you the itinerary for Russia."

"Thank you, sir," Ben said.

"Do you think I should be here?" Mishka asked.

"No. I see no reason to put you out there. I'm not losing you to some homophobic Banetti."

239

"So, I'm no longer in charge?" Mishka didn't know whether to be relieved or insulted. Was his father retaking his position as boss again? If he wanted to remove Mishka, there wouldn't be a fight from him since he really didn't want to deal with some of the criminals.

"You'll be in charge when I call you back home. I don't want to work anymore so you're not getting out of your position. Take some time to get to know Ben. You haven't been on a vacation for four years. You work all day and night and need a break so you can return with a new perspective. This is well deserved. Enjoy it."

"How long will we be gone?" Ben asked.

"Maybe a couple of weeks. Things should be settled when you have to return to Columbia University. I'll make sure you don't miss a day, Ben. I know you worked hard and this is important to you."

"Thank you, sir. I appreciate everything you're doing to help us," Ben said.

"Don't leave the house. I ordered more security. I'll be back when Jasha and Kylan come home." He hugged both of them, and kissed them on their cheeks.

Once he left, Mishka studied the sadness crawling across Ben's face. It had to hurt him that his father didn't care someone had placed a hit on him. No question, Sal was an unreasonable man.

"Ben, are you okay?"

"I don't know what I am at the moment. Hearing my father upset me. He's damn thick headed. He was always that way. No matter what, he'll side with my brothers and Dante before me. He always ignored me. I was sent away to school, and in the summer I stayed with my grandparents. My father took my brothers and Dante many places unrelated to business without me. I would have gone, but he never invited me. I don't know how to feel now. Either way, someone is going to die."

"I don't like it either. But as I mentioned, my father will always find a peaceful solution if he can. He upped the ante with your father, but he knows what he's doing. Money motivates Sal, but I'm sure you know that. He's not a good father, Ben. But mine will be a better one for you. Let him love you. He will." Mishka kissed Ben.

"I know he will be better than my father," Ben said.

"I'm looking forward to having a vacation, we'll have a lot of time to get to know each other in so many delicious ways. But I don't like leaving my father with this mess. He's a peaceful negotiator, so if there is a way to fix this, he'll fix it. Of course, my first instinct would be to take out your family."

"Then I guess you need to learn more skills from your father."

"He wants to stay illegal, and I want all my clubs legal and some other things too."

"My family has been working with drugs and prostitution forever. I never was interested in taking drugs because it makes me sick from all the violence that comes with it."

BRINA BRADY

CHAPTER TWENTY-FOUR

Ben

Ben woke up to Mishka carrying coffee into their bedroom. He strolled in as if he owned the world. Their eyes met for a brief moment. Mishka's lips curled into a smile as he stood there in jeans and a buttoned-up shirt. He handed Ben a mug of coffee and sat beside him with his.

"Thanks."

"Are you upset about us hiding away?"

"I'd like my freedom back someday, but I think it might be a time for us to be alone."

"Not totally alone. Jasha and Kylan would be with us."

"I don't mind them hanging out with us as long as we have some time for us."

"Do you and Kylan have passports?"

"Yes, we both just renewed ours."

"That's good. You never know when you're going to need one."

After they finished their coffee, Ben got up and planned to take a shower. He didn't get far when Mishka had pressed him against the wall.

244

"Take my cock." Mishka unzipped his jeans, put on a condom, and slowly slid his cock in and out of his hole. Whimpering and moans escaped from Ben's mouth. Mishka tightened his arm around his waist and gripped his hip to hold him steady. Ben arched his back for Mishka, but the stretch of his hole was a little sore.

"You've got such a hungry hole, boy."

Suddenly, Ben's hole tightened when Mishka continued to slide his cock in and out, fucking him. With Mishka's body weight against Ben's back, his hot breath in his ear, he whispered, "My cock is where it belongs. Your ass was made for me. Just relax and enjoy me."

He used the same firm but gentle voice when they had sex in bed. Ben slowed his breathing and relaxed his ass muscles the best he could. Mishka gave him a few more seconds to adjust before he moved again. He slowly thrust and filled him, inch by inch going deeper. Every part of Ben screamed with delight. Mishka stopped moving, and Ben realized he had settled in as deep as he could go. He had given Ben all of his cock.

"You're mine, Ben. All mine."

"I want to be yours and only yours, Sir," Ben panted.

Every time Mishka pushed his cock into Ben, it punched his prostate, sending an amazing feeling to his balls.

Mishka slammed his cock inside him, and his special spot ignited a fire of desire inside him. He rocked his body and moved with Mishka, who slipped his hand under Ben and rubbed his cock. Ben wanted this delightful feeling to last forever, but in seconds, he blasted his cum onto Mishka's hand, who continued pumping until he came as well, spilling his cum into the condom.

***

"The limo picked up Jasha and Kylan early this morning and they should be here soon. Are you getting excited about visiting Russia?" Mishka asked.

"Yes," Ben said.

"Put on something comfortable because I don't know what's going to happen today," Mishka suggested.

After Ben showered and dressed, he went to the living area where he heard Kylan talking to Mishka.

"Hey, where's Jasha?" Ben asked.

"He's in bed right now until my father shows up with what's next," Mishka said.

"Ben, are you okay with going to Russia?" Kylan asked.

"Sure. I've always wanted to go there."

"Me too," Kylan said.

Within a few hours, the four of them were packed and on a plane to Moscow. Shurik had purchased them first class seats so the flight was pleasant. Poor Jasha did a lot of sleeping and Kylan read a book on his iPad. Mishka and Ben were wide-awake so they had time to talk.

"My father has a home in a wooded area near Moscow. My aunt Emma went grocery shopping for us. He doesn't want us out and about for a few days."

"So we'll be locked in the house?"

"We'll find things to do in the woods. But after a few days, we can tour the area."

When they landed at the airport, they had a van take them away from the city to a small town in the woods. The house was pushed back from the main streets. It was the perfect hideout. Once they entered the house, Mishka showed Kylan and Jasha to their rooms. Ben followed Mishka to their bedroom. It was a fair size bedroom decorated with very frilly and homemade items. They unpacked their suitcases and when they were done, moved to the living room. Ben thought it was odd Jasha and Kylan didn't show up at the common area. He wondered if they had planned to sleep in the same room, not that it was any of his business.

"This home originally belonged to my grandparents on my father's side. They raised my father and his sister here. My father left Russia when he was twenty to start his own businesses."

"Is this home still in your family when no one lives here?"

"Some of our relatives come here for vacation."

"It makes a good hideaway, too," Ben said.

After a few days of doing not much more than wandering the woods, eating, talking, and sleeping, Mishka told Ben it was time to discover Russia. Jasha and Kylan had decided to take a trip to Moscow the day before so they had a head start. Last night, Mishka and Ben had packed their suitcases ready to go into the city.

The chilly morning arrived soon enough. Ben sat up in bed and looked through the window, noting how hard the wind blew the trees. His only thought was how they would get to the city. Ben rubbed his cold feet against Mishka, trying to wake him up.

"Ben, stop rubbing your cold feet on me." Mishka kicked Ben lightly.

"We have a major problem with all the damn rain," Ben said.

"We're in Russia and it rains here too. What's wrong?" Mishka turned over to face Ben.

"Look outside." Ben rubbed his legs to warm them again.

"Fuck! These crazy winds might cancel our trip to Sochi."

"How the hell are we going to get to the Vnukovo International Airport in this storm?" Ben asked.

"I'll call for a van to take us there." Mishka picked up his phone on the end table. He turned it on, then slammed it down. "I don't have a signal. Check your phone."

Ben checked his phone. "Nothing. Now what?"

"Go make some coffee for us. I'll try to work something out."

"Yes, Sir."

"You know you tease my cock when you call me Sir." Mishka sat up in bed and propped two pillows behind him.

"Yes, Sir." Ben threw on his gray sweats and a pair of matching socks.

He entered the kitchen and made coffee for both of them. He was more than grateful that Mishka's aunt Emma planned ahead and stocked food and supplies in the house.

249

It was too bad she had a trip planned and couldn't visit with them. He peeked through the kitchen window, almost blinded by the lightning. Mishka came up behind him, his arms locking around Ben's waist; his breath was warm and moist against his face and Ben's heart raced. He had no desire to break out of his embrace. He brushed a tender kiss on Ben's neck, sending chills up his spine.

"What's taking you so long with my coffee, boy?" Mishka teased.

Ben turned around, and pressed his lips against Mishka's. His skin tingled from the embrace. Mishka's hands traveled inside Ben's sweats and pinched his ass cheek.

"It's done now." Ben pushed away from Mishka. "Do you suppose we'll still be here for breakfast?"

Mishka nodded. "Yes."

"Do you want me to cook some eggs and bacon?" Ben asked.

"No, I want to cook today. You sit down and drink your coffee." Mishka poured coffee in a mug for Ben and handed it to him.

Ben sat down, sipped his coffee, and enjoyed watching Mishka frying the bacon for them. He was all his now, regardless of where they were. He didn't have to share him with anyone, which brought him comfort.

"Do you ever miss your life before you took over from your father?" Ben got up and poured them each a glass of orange juice and stuck two pieces of bread into the toaster.

"I do, but I'm not feeling good about my father taking care of something I should be." Mishka scrambled the eggs in a cast iron pan.

"He has a more peaceful approach to the problem, plus he knows my father better than you do. And you need a vacation," Ben said.

"I miss being a mobster's son instead of being the mobster boss. The further away I am from it tells me I wasn't meant to do what my father does."

"Do you think you could ever walk away?"

"I'd rather turn all my businesses to be on the right side of the law." Mishka filled each of their plates with eggs and bacon.

"I think you can do it. If you're the boss, then make it happen. As far as my father, he doesn't need your clubs to sell drugs and prostitutes. Get rid of my family." Ben buttered the toast and set them on a plate on the table.

"You're very intelligent and challenge my way of thinking sometimes," Mishka admitted.

"I want you to achieve what you want, and I believe you can do it."

"You can help me get there." Mishka smiled.

"I'm here for you. Why hasn't your father called?"

"He's working on the Banetti problem. The silence indicates he's in waiting mode." Mishka sat down across from Ben.

"Waiting for what?"

"For your father to call him with some more information. I'm sure he's looking into it."

After breakfast, Ben washed the dishes while Mishka showered. When Mishka was all dressed, Ben took his shower and after, they met in the little living room.

"Were you able to call anyone?" Ben asked.

"No, come and sit down by the fire with me," Mishka said.

Ben sat down beside Mishka, who wrapped a blanket around them in front of the large crackling fireplace.

"What's going to happen?" Ben asked.

"Nothing. We'll wait for the storm to end."

"I finally have your attention." Ben glanced at Mishka coyly. Mishka had been on many phone calls during their stay at the house.

"And what do you want with my attention?" Mishka asked.

"Just being here with you all to myself is enough."

"I think this is the perfect time to discuss BDSM. We're finally alone."

"I'd like to talk about BDSM with you."

"What does a BDSM relationship mean to you?" Mishka asked.

"Two people meet each other's sexual needs by an exchange of power. The sub gives up his power to his Dom. He protects his sub and the sub gives permission for the Dom to direct him."

"Close enough. Right now, we're practicing domestic discipline. I make the rules and you follow them in turn for my protection and care. If you break the rules, you get a whipping."

"I'm real careful with your rules, Sir. I don't want you angry at me anymore."

"But sometimes, you like me to spank you, don't you?"

"Yes, I love when you spank me, but not when you're angry with me."

"We'll work on more spankings that make you feel good."

"Can we do some scenes?" Ben asked.

"Do you mean practice some scenes without being my sub?" Mishka asked.

"I've never had a Dom on contract, and I've done some scenes at clubs. I want you to do a scene with me in your playroom, or even here."

"Before we do any scenes, I'll need to find out what you want and don't want to do. As the Dom, I create the scenes."

"How about a checklist?"

"I don't have one of my own since I've never had a permanent sub. There's a list in the BDSM book, so, I'll retype and have you fill it out. You could use the traffic light model for your safewords while we're playing."

"Anything else?"

"During a scene, you are to address me as Sir," Mishka said.

"Yes, Sir. I really want you to be my Dom."

"You're not ready for that yet. I told you that you need to trust me first. I don't see enough signs of that yet."

"Can't you give me a trust test then?" Ben asked.

"There are some tests for trust, but I prefer to watch you and see how you interact with me."

"So, I'm not sub material?"

254

"Not at this time, but we can play when we get home."

"Why not here?"

"I'll think about it."

Ben wondered why Mishka was so reluctant to play with him. He had that awesome playroom, but said he'd never used it. Something wasn't adding up as to why he was in no rush.

CHAPTER TWENTY-FIVE

Mishka

They arrived in the late afternoon at their hotel room in Sochi. Jasha and Kylan were in another room on the same floor, having arrived earlier.

"So what do you think of Sochi?" Mishka asked.

"I love the Black Sea and the amusement area. It reminds me of Wildwood's boardwalk. Do you go on any of the rides?" Ben asked.

"I love rides especially the roller coaster. Are you ready to go out to dinner?"

"I'm ready."

Mishka claimed Ben's lips, crushing their lips together.

"I can't get enough of you, Ben."

Once they arrived at the restaurant, they sat outside under an umbrella facing the Black Sea. The scenery was breathtaking. Ben seemed to love Russia and he was delighted speaking Russian everywhere they'd gone. He knew more Russian with perfect pronunciations than Mishka and Jasha. They hadn't studied it, but learned from their parents. It was so odd, but Ben fit right in with the Chernov family, probably better than he had in his own

256

family. It didn't seem like anyone in the Banetti family appreciated Ben. He was so knowledgeable and creative. How could his family mistreat him?

The hotel restaurant was so lavish that the prices weren't on the menu. Mishka was relieved Ben seemed impressed. When the server came to their table, Mishka ordered prime rib, medium rare. Ben ordered the same, but explained he wanted everything on the side and to make sure his meat wasn't overcooked. Mishka listened to the firm command in Ben's voice as he ordered with absolute precision of what he wanted and how he wanted it served, all in perfect Russian. Ben also ordered wine for them.

When the server brought the wine he'd requested to the table, he tasted it first. Wine was not important to Mishka—he only drank it to be polite. He had no idea how to determine the classification of the wine he sipped until Ben informed him. According to his father, Ben's family grew their own grapes and even had a wine room at his home. Ben explained the basics of how to grow grapes and make wine, but much of it went in one ear and out the other. Mishka decided he did want to learn more about the categories and classifications of wine though, since Ben thought it was important to a meal.

"I don't know how long we'll be here," Mishka said.

257

"I know, but what if something has happened to your father?" Ben asked.

"He's fine, Ben. He just doesn't want me calling him while he's working with Sal for some damn reason."

"You still lucked out with a better father than I did." Ben sipped his wine.

"I agree. Once things are settled, we'll be able to go out anytime we want."

Kylan and Jasha found them drinking wine.

"Hey, do you mind if we join you two?" Jasha asked, when he and Kylan approached them.

Mishka wanted to have dinner alone with Ben, but he couldn't say no. "Sure, sit down."

The server immediately took their order so their food would be served at the same time. Ben poured wine into their glasses.

"When did you guys get here?" Kylan asked.

"Two hours ago," Mishka said.

"I have something to announce," Jasha said, looking a little nervous.

"Announce?" Mishka asked.

"This isn't easy for me to tell you. I've thought about it, and Kylan told me I didn't have anything to fear so…

I'm gay and… Kylan and I are a thing." Jasha's face reddened and Kylan smiled at him with approval.

Ben looked at Kylan and Mishka looked at Jasha. Both had no words.

"So, why are you guys so silent?" Kylan asked.

"Shocked, that's all. I'm happy my brother found someone to make him happy." Mishka got up and hugged Jasha. "Damn, I really am happy for you."

"Well, it's about time you found someone, Kylan," Ben said.

"Let's drink to Jasha and Kylan." Mishka lifted his wine glass and they smiled when they clinked glasses to celebrate Jasha and Kylan's new relationship.

Mishka looked at Kylan in a different way for the first time. He no longer viewed him as competition for Ben's attention. He truly was relieved he'd found someone. As for Jasha, he was shocked about him coming out as gay. He shouldn't have been surprised since he'd never dated a girl. Still, he wondered why it took him so long to admit—or figure out—he was gay. He must have been so confused. Now, Jasha had a special person in his life for the first time. He loved Jasha and he thought Kylan would protect Jasha in every way so he'd be safe, but looking at them, they were happy and that's all that mattered in the end.

After dinner, they separated; with Mishka and Ben taking a walk along the beach. They didn't hold hands because it wasn't accepted here. Not that it was accepted everywhere back home either and some areas were definitely safer than others.

***

The next day, Mishka's phone woke him out of a dead sleep. Ben woke up too.

"Hope all is well in Sochi," Shurik said.

"We're fine. So, what happened?"

"You guys can come home. I made a deal with Sal. He banished Dante and his older son Freddie. They were moved to Sicily."

"And what's the part you're not saying?"

"I signed one club over to him and his family is out of our clubs forever. You'll have all legal clubs. From there, you can move your other areas the way you want. This way, Sal is happy and so are you. Although, he's a broken man over the betrayal of Freddie and Dante."

"Where does that leave Ben with Sal?"

"Nothing has changed. I'm sorry for Ben, but Sal is a bastard and he raised a son who plotted to kill his own brother. So, it's time for you to return and take over."

"Thanks, Dad. You're the best. I know I couldn't have made a deal with Sal. So, you're saying I never have to deal with him?"

"That's right. So, come home."

"We'll be there as soon as we can. I'll send you a message with our return information. Have the driver pick us up at LaGuardia."

"I'm looking forward to all my sons returning home."

"Love you, Dad."

"I love you too." He ended the call.

"What did he say?" Ben asked.

"We can go home. Your father banished Freddie and Dante to Sicily. I guess he found out what they did to you and Kylan. My father made a deal with one of the clubs and now we don't have to deal with any Banetti, ever again."

"Any Banetti?" Ben asked.

"I'm not talking about you."

"I'm a Banetti, Mishka."

"I'm sorry, it came out wrong. I meant all the other ones except my precious Ben."

"So, my father sent Freddie and Dante on a vacation to Sicily for attempting to kill Kylan and me?" Ben punched the wall so hard his knuckles bled. "That fucking bastard! He basically rewarded them."

261

"Ben, you're bleeding," Mishka got up and went through his bag in the bathroom. He returned with a wet washcloth, wiped the back of Ben's hand, and put a Band-Aid on it.

"Thanks. I'm just so damn angry at him."

"I know. At least he knows who fucked up and who didn't."

"But he rewarded them." Ben's face turned red.

"It feels that way, but you don't know what will happen in Sicily."

"What do you mean?" Ben asked.

"He might have someone take them out there away from the family. This way he can wash his hands of it."

"He'd never do that to Freddie or Dante. He values their lives more than mine."

"I'm going to send a text to Jasha that we're leaving tomorrow. We'll have to hit the rides today."

"I guess it's safe enough for me to move back to my Wildwood condo," Ben said.

"Move? You won't go back home," Mishka said.

"I don't need your protection so I can go home," Ben stated.

Mishka couldn't believe his ears. Why would Ben leave him? He didn't understand why he would want to leave. Did he only pretend he had wanted to be with him?

"So all this time, you fucking used me for your protection? And now, you don't need my help, you're leaving? What kind of fucking game are you playing?" Mishka picked up a lamp and threw it against the wall. "You sold your ass to me for my protection. Everything you said to me was just a little con. I should have known there weren't any decent Banetti men. You're just another fucked up Banetti."

Ben's face paled from Mishka's words. "I never conned you, Mishka. You just assumed I'd move in permanently with you. I never planned on living with you. That doesn't mean I'm fucked up and I don't want to—"

Mishka cut Ben right off and talked over him. "Just shut up, Benito. And yes, you are fucked up. I don't want another Banetti asshole around me anyway. That's what you are. You led me on and that won't happen again."

Ben said nothing. Obviously it was a sign he was done with him forever. Kylan had said Ben fought for what he wanted and apparently, Mishka wasn't who he wanted because he didn't deny anything.

263

At four in the morning, Mishka dressed in silence. He left Ben in bed and slammed the door on his way out. He walked the beach hurting from the pain of Ben playing him for a fool. None of this made sense. He was ready to commit to Ben in every way, and eventually, he wanted to make Ben his sub if he had agreed. All his future plans with Ben had been blown up by one fucking sentence. *I don't need your protection so I can go home.*

Mishka couldn't return to the room and he certainly didn't want to see Ben anymore. He was done. *No one fucks with me. He's a damn Banetti.*

He called Jasha.

"What's up?"

"Ben is moving back to Wildwood. I can't believe he played me like this."

"Wait. Maybe he wants to recover from what's happened with his family. I can't believe he wants to break up with you," Jasha said.

Mishka heard Kylan in the background asking questions.

"Kylan wants to talk to you," Jasha said.

"Sure, put him on."

"What happened?" Kylan asked.

"I told Ben about the deal and what his father did to Freddie and Dante. He told me he doesn't need me anymore, and he was moving back to Wildwood."

"Ben's hurting now. Sal showed how little he valued his life. He wants to go home to something familiar to regroup. But he needs you. Give him a little space. I'll be with him and make sure he heals. It's not over for him. There's no way his healing period will last more than a week. I can guarantee it."

"Tell Jasha to book two separate flights. You go with Ben and Jasha will be with me. He's in my room now. Have him out of the room at noon so I can get my things. I'm going to get another room for the night."

"Don't you think you should fly with him?" Kylan asked.

"No. I don't want to be near him right now. He can have all the fucking space he wants."

"I'll handle it. The room will be empty at noon," Kylan said. "You have to let him grieve."

"He can fucking grieve the rest of his pathetic life. Thanks."

CHAPTER TWENTY-SIX

Ben

Ben sat tapping his right foot and chewing at his nails while he waited for Mishka to return. His eyes darted back and forth between the phone and the door; why can't time tick any faster? He stood and paced back and forth, pulling at his shirt. He ran his hands through his hair, while stealing a peek at the time on his phone. Only thirty minutes had passed since Mishka had left. Ben sat down again on his bed. The sounds of the waves hitting the sand was soothing, reminding him of Wildwood. Ben felt like he was the only one awake, pacing back and forth in the early morning. He couldn't believe he'd only been waiting thirty minutes.

A few hours later, Kylan knocked on the door and Ben let him in.

"What's going on, Ben?" Kylan asked.

"Mishka never returned. He left early this morning."

"Something must have made him leave." Kylan raised his brows.

"I told him I was moving back to my condo. I guess he thought I'd stay with him."

266

"Why wouldn't you stay with him?"

"I don't want to be a part of his world."

"His world? Ben, you are his world. You knew who he was and now you don't want him? You were disowned because you wanted to be with him."

"I can't deal with anymore thugs."

"Do you really think he's a thug?"

"His family does shit that's against the law. I can't be a part of it. It's my family all over again. I want to go home, be alone to think."

"That's fucking bullshit, Ben. He's told you he's changing the business so everything can be legitimate," Kylan said.

"I know he did. It's not really about that. I'm so upset I'm talking shit about the mess I made."

"What changed?"

"I'm tired of Mishka's mixed messages. He treats me like a sub, but I'm not good enough to be his sub. I don't know what he wants and I'm tired of waiting for him to tell me. I just need some time to myself."

"I think you're not telling me the entire story."

"I can't right now. All I know is I want you to continue working as my security."

"Of course, I go where you go. Here's a copy of your electronic ticket for New York as a backup. I forwarded your e-ticket to your email too." Kylan pulled out a paper and handed it to him.

"Do you know where Mishka is?" Ben asked.

"He rented another room."

"He's done with me, I guess." Ben didn't want to break up with Mishka. He hadn't meant he never wanted to see Mishka again. Why couldn't they date? Did they have to live together? Ben eventually wanted to live with Mishka, but not right now. He had to get to grip on his emotions. If Mishka loved him, he wouldn't have left him in a hotel room—alone—in a foreign country. Mishka might have had feelings for him, but their love wasn't strong enough to make him want to stay and work things out. The lines of communication had broken down with Mishka, and now Ben felt a sense of longing, unease, and even bitterness.

Mishka's so-called protection didn't include loving Ben deeply and intensely enough as Ben had thought. Their first disagreement and Mishka had no problem leaving him and insulting him and his family. He should have known Mishka hated all Banetti men, including Ben. He had to face it—Mishka never loved him at all. He was just a hole to stick his cock in, the same cock that he shoved up Ben's ass in the Crowbar alley. He should have expected as much from a Chernov. His father hated them and maybe there was good reason for that. Yet, he thought about how kind and loving Mr. Chernov was. No, there was nothing wrong with the Chernovs, just Mishka. His protection was worthless when Ben was broken emotionally from his father's rejection. He needed understanding at this time, not insults to deepen his wounds.

"Ben, you told him you wanted to go home." Kylan's words snapped Ben out of his wretched thoughts.

"I do want to go home, but I didn't mean I never wanted to see him again. He got so pissed at me and shit went down. There was nothing I could do or say to stop him."

"Did he hurt you?" Kylan asked.

"Not the way you think. He said some horrible things to me, and he wouldn't let me explain."

"You had your first fight with Mishka, and it won't be your last."

"Why are you here anyway?" Ben asked, not wanting to discuss what Mishka had said. The hurt from their conversation was too much to deal with.

"I want to take you to lunch."

269

"Lunch?" Ben hadn't eaten breakfast.

"Come on. Jasha is meeting a relative so I didn't want to eat alone in the room. Would you go with me?"

"Sure." Ben owed his life to Kylan so he couldn't very well say no.

They left the room and made their way to the amusement area. Kylan was always his partner to go on the rides in Wildwood. They stopped to ride the roller coaster. After they had ridden a few other rides, they stopped for lunch.

"Are we going to talk about what happened between you and Mishka?" Kylan asked as he sat done.

"I already told you that he left the room when I told him I wanted to live in Wildwood. I guess he thought I'd live with him forever."

"Well, what do you have to lose by staying with him?"

"I'm not saying I don't ever want to see him. Mishka doesn't really want me as much as I wanted him. I don't want to be devastated when he leaves."

"You're not making any sense. You're the one who fucked up here. What more does Mishka have to do for you to show he loves you? Why couldn't you tell him you wanted to see him, but needed some time alone?"

"I don't know. I fucked up."

When he returned to the room, Ben immediately noticed Mishka's suitcases were gone. He had left without saying a word. He looked around for a note, but there wasn't one. What did he expect? Ben's emotions ran all over the place, missing Mishka, but at the same time, wanting to go home alone. Mishka had played too many games with him. All Ben wanted was to be nothing more than a boyfriend to him. He didn't want to need his protection. He wanted a Dom, a real one. Mishka didn't think Ben qualified as a sub. His excuse had been Ben didn't trust him. What was there to trust? He'd dumped him in a foreign country and called him names. He could have stayed and discussed what Ben had wanted. He walked away from him, and that said it all.

When the morning came, Ben hadn't slept at all because as stupid as it was, he still was waiting for Mishka to return and say he was sorry for leaving. Kylan picked him up, and they took a cab to the airport.

"Where's Jasha?" Ben asked.

"He's on another flight with Mishka."

"What? Mishka isn't going to be on the same flight?" Ben tightened his jaw to ward off tears. Of course, the total rejection had hurt him in places he didn't know existed. The shock of defeat held him immobile.

271

"Ben, you hurt him."

"Let's go." Ben was pissed at himself for hurting Mishka. Maybe he could have used different words to explain what he needed. No one understood he needed some space to be alone to think.

"Are you okay?" Kylan asked.

"I'm fine. Just fine," Ben said.

Ben slept most of the way on the flight. Once they arrived in New York, they took a shuttle to Wildwood. Ben was miserable without Mishka. What the hell was he thinking? He wanted to be with him, but in his own home. He needed to feel like himself again, but he needed to find who he was... or used to be. Whoever he was right now was uncomfortable and unfamiliar.

When they arrived at the condo, Kylan refused to leave him alone so he stayed in the guest room. Ben worried Kylan had wanted to spend time with Jasha, and now Ben had fucked everyone's trip with his announcement to move back home. All he really wanted was to touch base at his home, get a sense he was going to be okay, and life would go on.

The doorbell rang. Ben checked the peephole and two men stood there carrying Kylan's and his things from Mishka's house. As he opened the door, intense pain burst in his stomach. Seeing his suitcases was a visible sign Mishka was done with him. That hurt him because Mishka mattered. Ben told himself the pain would pass, that life would go on, but in that moment, he didn't believe that. The pain clouded his vision as it filled his emotional world. The pain was all there was.

"We're returning your things from Mr. Chernov's place," the shorter man said.

"Thank you. You can put them there." Ben pointed to the empty space beside the recliner.

After Ben gave them a large tip, they left without a message from Mishka. Ben stared at his things and felt depressed for ruining the best thing in his life.

Kylan picked up his suitcase. "I guess he's done with you."

"I guess so."

"Is that what you wanted, Ben?"

"I don't know. I'm lost without him."

"Why don't you call him? Tell him how you feel," Kylan suggested.

"I don't know how I feel. I miss him, but I don't want to move in with him."

"Tell him that. Let him know you're still interested and care about him. Think about how he feels."

273

Ben carried his laptop with him to his bedroom. He sat down on the bed and called Mishka. His cell went to voicemail, so he sent a text instead of leaving a pitiful voicemail.

Ben: *I'm sorry if I hurt you by wanting to go home. I miss you. Please call me.*

Of course, Mishka didn't want to talk to Ben after he'd pretty much told him to fuck himself now that he didn't need his protection. Was that what he had done? He wanted Mishka, but he didn't want it to be from the aspect of Ben needing him for protection; he wanted to be on equal footing with him. He didn't know what to do. He could visit him, but he might not answer the door. Ben had created his own nightmare and he had no idea how to fix the chaos he had caused. If he'd never met Mishka in the first place, none of the mess would have happened. Maybe he should have married his cousin as his father had suggested. But he wanted Mishka. Ben's thoughts wouldn't shut off, constantly going in circles without any solutions. He couldn't breathe with the heaviness that came over him.

Ben called his mother. "Mom, this is Ben. I'm okay. Are you still in Florida?"

"Yes. Your father and I decided not to live together anymore after he sent Freddie and Dante away. He should
274

have known what was going on before they tried to hurt you. I blame him. He allowed your brothers to hate you. He never said anything because he was the instigator and leader of their bully brigade."

"I knew he didn't approve of my lifestyle, but I never thought they would want me dead."

"Your father didn't want you dead. Freddie did though. He got Dante to do the dirty work for him. Instead of your father being upset for what they did to you, he's more upset his favorite son Freddie betrayed him."

"Mom, it was always all about him and no one else. I'm glad you left him. He doesn't deserve you."

"I heard you were okay and happy with Mishka."

"I'm fine. I just wanted to see how you were doing."

"Did Mishka tell you his mother used to visit me in Florida?"

"Yes, he did. What kind of person was she?" Ben asked.

"She was a lot of fun. We used to go out and have the best of times. I miss her. I'd love for you and Mishka to visit me here in Florida."

"I'll talk to him about that."

"I'm so happy you followed your heart. Your father is miserable. He knows he shouldn't have disowned you."

"Well, he did."

"I have a feeling he wants you back."

"No thanks. As long as I have you, I'm good."

BRINA BRADY

CHAPTER TWENTY-SEVEN

Mishka

Mishka missed Ben, but it was over because Ben said it was. He'd wanted to move back home because he didn't need Mishka's protection anymore. Mishka had felt the pain of Ben's words when he had spoken them. Each time Mishka thought about Ben lying beside him in bed, the pain of their separation deepened. Jasha stayed with him since Kylan was with Ben. Maybe Ben had wanted Kylan all along and both of them used him. Mishka knew that wasn't true, but those thoughts made him suffer more because he deserved to suffer for fucking things up with Ben.

Mishka had never felt anything like this before. He'd been to the damn depths of hell and back, yet he didn't believe it would hurt as badly as it had. Somehow, his heart had been torn apart. Not crushed, not shattered, but torn. Ripped. Mishka had given Ben a piece of his heart, and he walked away without returning it. Everyone expected him to keep going, despite the fact part of him was missing.

Mishka turned the blame to himself. Just thinking about Ben stopped his normal breathing. It had to be Mishka's fault for caring about Ben when he had entered

278

his life needing him without wanting him. There never was a chance for a Banetti and Chernov to unite as they had.

Jasha was watching a movie while Mishka stared at the wall. Finally, Jasha found someone and now he wasn't with his lover. He'd been too worried about Mishka. No one should worry about him. He was the boss. Bosses didn't get hurt. Bosses shouldn't give a fuck and that's where Mishka went wrong.

"Mishka, it's been a week. Why don't you call Ben and talk to him?" Jasha asked.

"Why would I do that? He doesn't want anything I can offer him." Mishka hurt more than he wanted to admit to himself and certainly never to anyone else.

"I talked to Kylan and he said Ben is miserable without you."

"And who's fault is that? Not mine. He's the one that walked away. I don't trust him anymore. He used me and played me."

"Give him a break! He thinks his father doesn't value him as a person. He's mixed up and hurting."

"He can fuck himself. I'm done." Mishka, once again, pulled his phone out ready to delete the message he'd received from Ben.

Ben: *Mishka, I'm sorry if I hurt you by wanting to go home. I miss you. Please call me.*

Mishka's heart softened for a moment for Ben in his fucked up world. He had said he was sorry, but what did that mean? He was sorry, he wants to move in, or he was sorry, he's not moving back? What was he sorry about? Then to make Mishka feel worse, Ben said he missed him. If he had missed him so much, why did he leave him just because he didn't need his protection anymore?

For Mishka, the separation from Ben resembled death. Food he had attempted to eat became tasteless. His sleep became fractured without a full night's rest. It was impossible to escape the shadow of Ben's presence. It was truly like Ben's ghost haunted him. His thoughts about Ben were always present; he was unable to push them away. Mishka rarely felt heartbroken after the end of a relationship, but with Ben leaving him, he wanted to stay in bed and isolate from others.

He couldn't find any comfort in those who cared about both of them. He wasn't about to mention his pain and sadness to his father. He had been like a father to Ben, and he'd thrown it all away. Ben turned out to be a man without respect or loyalty for the Chernov family.

They had shared a very intimate and loving bond and Mishka had committed himself to Ben fully; to lose him so suddenly hurt in places he didn't know existed. Was Ben ever present in their relationship or was he using Mishka as a means to his end their entire time together?

The idea of exploring other men was absolutely repulsive. He was destined to be alone, and he'd better get used to it. He missed Ben, he was so perfect for him, and now he would be perfect for someone else. He didn't believe that his memories with Ben would ever go away. Mishka missed himself with Ben. He missed who Ben made him become. He became alive. He became ecstatic; enchanted; jubilant. Mishka became the best form of himself. And then out of nowhere, Mishka lost himself. Suddenly, he became a person that he wasn't familiar with. He couldn't keep a solid thought and his body ached for sleep.

Did Ben leave him to return to the Banetti family? Would Sal take Ben back into the fold? The only good thing that came out of this mess was his father had gotten rid of the Banetti family in his clubs. He had many other areas to clean up, and he would work on them.

"Why don't you take a ride to Ben's condo?" Jasha asked.

281

"I see no reason to visit him when he clearly doesn't want to live with me," Mishka said.

"Can't you see him and make the case to him?" Jasha asked.

"He's been with me. There shouldn't be a case to sell to him. I think he wants his father to take him back. That's probably why he left me."

"Mishka, he loves you. I can see it in his eyes. He's a little hurt right now. Go to him."

"Oh, you want me to go there so you can see Kylan, right? I don't blame you."

"You're so damn thick headed. You always were. I know you want to see him. Fight for him. Isn't he worth it?" Jasha asked.

"I don't know if I could see him without cursing him out for what he did."

"Stay alone then." Jasha walked away from Mishka.

Without any knocking, his father barged into the living room.

"I heard little Ben is gone. What went wrong?" his father demanded.

"I don't know. Once he found out he was safe, he wanted to move back home."

"And you let him?"

282

"That's his choice."

"Why didn't all four of you take the same flight?"

"I didn't want to see him after he had told me he wanted to leave."

"You were happy with him. He left his family for you. And you just let him go. Fight for him."

"Who told you about this?" Mishka asked.

"It doesn't matter. My advice is to go to Wildwood. Stay with him and talk your differences out until you find an agreement you both can endure. I sure failed at teaching you how to negotiate."

Jasha came in when they were talking. "I have something to tell you, Dad," Jasha said.

"Something good, I hope."

"Depends. I found out that I'm gay."

"So now I have three gay sons. Okay? Must be a trend these days." Shurik hugged Jasha. "I think I knew when you never brought home a girl. I love you, Jasha, no matter what."

"Thanks, Dad. I have something else to tell you too."

"More?"

"I'm seeing Kylan."

"Kylan! You couldn't have found a better man. At least I know you'll be safe with him. He's a good man. So, I'll have four sons now."

"Thanks for being you, Dad," Jasha said.

"Yes, we have the best dad," Mishka said.

"How about you two take a trip to Wildwood and straighten things out?" Shurik suggested.

Within an hour, a limo picked up Mishka and Jasha set to go to Wildwood. It was at least a three-hour ride and the whole way, Mishka replayed different conversations in his mind so he could get it straight. He hoped he could make his case to Ben as Jasha had said. There was a possibility he would reject any offer he would suggest. Maybe Ben was hurting over his father disowning him and he had overreacted when Ben only needed healing time in his condo. It had to be more. He wanted to be his sub and Mishka continued to push him away. Now, he wondered if he had contributed to Ben's leaving because he didn't feel secure. Ben saw the playroom and did scenes and still he told Ben he wasn't ready. Mishka had a problem with giving mixed messages. He certainly shouldn't have said so many horrible things to him.

"What if he's not home?" Mishka asked Jasha.

"I told Kylan we're on our way."

"Why did you tell him that? He's not going to be there if he knows I'm on the way." Mishka closed his eyes so he wouldn't swear at Jasha for calling Kylan.

"I told him to make sure he stays home; he's not going to tell Ben that we're on the way. He said Ben hasn't been out of his condo since he got home. That's a week staying inside. He stays mostly in bed doing nothing. At least you went to work."

"It sounds like he's depressed." Mishka didn't feel like doing anything either although he did make the rounds at his clubs and spoke to his men. Ben didn't have the same responsibilities in the summer that Mishka had. He wasn't especially happy to hear how sad Ben was, but in a way, he hoped it helped his chances getting back with him. He didn't want to carry on without Ben.

"Here's the deal. Kylan and I are going to his condo so you two can be alone. Call me if you need anything."

"Thanks. I've missed him so much. I feel like I'm running on empty without him. I hope I can negotiate something so we can live together. And as you know, I suck at compromising."

"You always did. I remember it was always your way or the highway. Dad would step in and make you give up something to get what you wanted. He was always fair between us."

"Yes, he was. I wish I had his skills and his strength to deal with the Banetti family and others like them. I wished they were all dead."

"Now, that's something you should keep in your head and never share with Ben. Remember he's still a Banetti, and it doesn't matter his father disowned him. Dad thinks Sal will still try and make up with him."

"I sure hope not. I don't want anything to do with Sal."

"You might not, but Ben does. Sal is his father."

"I thought you hated the Banetti family after what they did to your parents?"

"I never said I liked the Banetti family, but Ben made you happy. He's not Sal."

BRINA BRADY

CHAPTER TWENTY-EIGHT

Ben

Ben stayed in bed longer than usual because he didn't want to do anything. His head throbbed from drinking too much last night. He reached for the aspirin bottle on the side dresser and took the pills with a bottle of water. Mishka never returned his message. Ben was too depressed to work out with Kylan. At some point Kylan would want to see Jasha and it wasn't fair to them that Kylan was stuck here with him. Ben hadn't expected the intense loneliness without Mishka at his side.

For hours Ben had tossed and turned in bed which meant he had slept enough. He took a long shower and put on a pair of jeans with a T-shirt. He heard Kylan talking on the phone. As soon as Ben entered the kitchen, he ended his conversation. No doubt he had been talking to Jasha and he didn't want Ben to know what they were talking about.

"Do you want something to eat since you haven't had a damn thing and it's four in the afternoon?"

"Kylan, you're my security guard not my mother, so you don't have to babysit me when I'm not going anywhere. You can see Jasha. I don't want to be the reason you're stuck here."

"Ben, I'm not stuck here. I want to be here with you. How about a grilled cheese and tomato soup?"

"I love your grilled cheese sandwiches. Thanks. That sounds good." Ben smiled for the first time since he'd been home. He didn't know what he'd do without Kylan.

Kylan warmed up the tomato soup and set it in a bowl for Ben. He placed saltines on the table. Ben had gotten a Gatorade to drink. Once Kylan cooked the grilled cheese, he put it on a plate for Ben, then sat down across from him.

"I thought we could put together that new bookshelf you ordered," Kylan said.

"Oh that's a good idea. I need to get that up. I have tons of books my mother had packed up and put in storage."

"I'm going to get some tools from my SUV."

Ben was cleaning up the kitchen when the doorbell rang. He wiped his hands and went to the door. He figured Kylan locked himself out. When he opened the door, he gasped. Mishka stood there looking delicious in his gray suit… matching his eyes perfectly. Exactly the sort of thing that a boss would wear. That was something that made him a bit nervous. Still, it fit well, it made him look very fine, and when he smiled, it traveled right down to Ben's balls.

"Well, are you going to invite me in?" Mishka asked.

"Sure. Come in." Ben suddenly realized how much he needed Mishka in his life right now.

Mishka entered the condo. "Wow! This is some condo—with an ocean view as well. I missed you, Ben."

"I missed you too."

"We need to talk about us and our future," Mishka said.

"Let's sit on the patio. Can I get you something to drink?"

Mishka pulled Ben close to him and kissed him. "I want you, Ben."

"I want you too."

Ben led Mishka to the kitchen and pulled out two bottled waters and then they moved to sit beside each other on the patio.

"Ben, why don't you want to live with me?"

"I want to be with you, but you're involved with illegal shit like my father."

"I'm not your father nor am I a Banetti. You really don't know what kind of businesses the Chernovs are invested in. They aren't all illegal. One by one, I'm cleaning them up. I've told you that so many times."

"What about the loan sharking?" Ben had heard his father discussing the Chernovs. That's how he found out what they had done.

"I got it down to fifty percent. I still have more work to do."

"What about the young girls and boys working the streets?"

"See, you don't know what you're talking about, Ben. My family stopped that a couple of years ago. We mostly do real estate and I own lots of clubs in New York."

"My father said your family traffics minors."

"Not true. Your father lies. So, you knew who I was, but you wanted me anyway. What changed?"

"I don't want to live my father's life."

"What about my father? Do you have any feelings for him in a fatherly way? He loves you like a son."

"I do care about your father and Jasha too."

"And do you just want me to fuck you and that's it? That's all you want me for?"

"I wanted to be your sub, but you acted like I wasn't capable. Each time I asked, you put me down. I wasn't good enough"

"So, now you left me because I wouldn't become your Dom?" Mishka asked.

"It's part of it. No one understands why I needed some space for myself. I'm a man without a family. I just thought if I went home, I would find myself again. That's what my leaving was really about and it didn't have anything to do with you. I left my family for you. I want you, but I needed to stay here. Can you understand that?"

"I get you needed to go home to something you know. I think you want your father to take you back into the family, or what's left of it at least. Did you once think about me in your decision?"

"I did think about you. I figured you were on the way to leaving me anyway since I wasn't good enough to be your sub. I'm sorry, I should have explained my feelings, but you walked out on me in a foreign country. Who does that?"

"I'm sorry I said cruel things to you. I didn't mean any of them. I was just hurt because all I heard was you were going home. We were over," Mishka said.

"I tried to explain, but you told me to shut up and when you started saying shit about how horrible I was, I just figured you were done with me."

"We have some major issues with our communication we need to work on. If you need to stay here, and I need to work in the city, which is over three hours away, how do you think we can have any type of relationship? I can't commute back and forth every day."

"What if you stayed with me here on the weekends?" Ben suggested.

"So, our relationship is worth only two days a week? Is that what you're suggesting?"

"I don't know how to make us work," Ben said.

"Do you want to be with me or not?" Mishka asked.

"I can't really function without you. I miss being with you, especially waking up to you. I don't know what I should do. Please make us work again."

"I'm going to make you a deal. Either you say yes or no. I don't want circular answering. Can you do that?"

"I'll try."

"Move back with me and I mean move everything you need. On the weekends, we can stay here. Kylan can be your security guard when you need him. When you need a day or so to yourself, tell me and get the space you need. If you do this, I'll begin training you to be a sub for me. When I think you know enough to commit to me as my sub, then I'll collar you. Yes or no, Ben?"

Ben stood up and looked out at the ocean and the beach. He didn't want to leave his home, but if he could live here on the weekends, he could do it. Apparently, he couldn't live without Mishka. Ben had missed the good times when he'd stayed with Mishka, but they ended in sad separation. But a discarded relationship certainly could have a do over. Basically the hurting words by both of them had divided them. Pain of separation had forced Ben to grow during their angered separation. Life was too short to allow selfishness rule over his life.

Ben turned around to face Mishka. "Yes."

"I love you, Ben. Don't you know that by now?"

"I love you too. I just never said that to anyone."

Mishka pulled Ben inside to the bedroom and stripped him of his clothes. Mishka hugged him and slipped his tongue into Ben's mouth, kissing him. Mishka's hands wandered all over his body, sending electricity everywhere they landed. Without warning, he pulled away from Ben, grinning at him. He shoved him onto the bed.

"Turn over," Mishka ordered.

Ben flipped over, as commanded. He waited while Mishka busied himself with removing his own clothes and setting up his lube and condom. When he returned to the bed, Mishka rubbed the outside area of Ben's tight hole.

294

Ben was rock hard against the sheets. He wanted Mishka inside.

"Stretch your hands above your head," Mishka ordered.

"Why?"

"Why what?"

"Why, Sir?"

"I'm going to cuff your hands to the headboard. Are you okay with that?"

"Yes, Sir." Ben realized Mishka must have thought he was good to go. This was what he wanted, pleasing his lover in every way. He trusted Mishka wouldn't hurt him or leave him alone.

"If you want me to remove the cuffs, what do you say?"

"Red, Sir."

Mishka clicked the red handcuff on his left hand to the bed, then he took his right hand, kissed it and cuffed it to the headboard too.

"These are from the Red Handcuffs and I thought we could play with them again."

"I remember, Sir."

Mishka rubbed Ben's bare butt with his finger, edging closer to his crack and then up and down it. Ben moaned.

295

Mishka entered him with one finger, stretching him. Ben felt the burn more when the second finger moved in. Ben arched to take more, but Mishka stopped and pulled his fingers out, leaving him empty. Mishka knew what he was doing all right. Ben moaned again as Mishka's finger circled his butt hole, teasing him with the promise of more. He pushed in just a little, driving Ben crazy with desire. He stopped to place a condom on, coating it with more lube.

"Relax," Mishka ordered.

His face and chest were flat on the bed. His ass was up, open to the cool air, the lube chilling his exposed hole. He wanted Mishka's cock inside of him… he had waited all week for this. How could he have left the man he loved? He couldn't make it without his love.

Mishka took his time admiring his lubed hole. He licked his ass-cheeks, biting and sucking them. "It still looks tight, I'm glad I bought the good lubricant."

"That's what happens when you don't play with me for a week."

Mishka smacked Ben's ass hard, igniting an intense interest in his balls.

"Do it again, Sir. Please."

Mishka didn't need to be asked twice. He smacked Ben's ass another five times consecutively. "That's for leaving me, you bad boy."

Ben figured he didn't want to hurt him too badly, but it felt good. The sting traveled to his balls, causing his cock to twitch and leak on the sheets. Having Mishka in his bed sure beat not having Mishka at all. Being alone, wishing the man he loved was here with him, sickened him.

Mishka returned his attention and his index finger to Ben's asshole. He slowly worked the length of his finger into Ben's ass. He added more lube and fingers, gently rotating them in and out. Ben's dick grew harder, another drop of pre-cum formed on his cockhead.

Mishka aimed his cock for his target; he pushed it in, going deeper with each thrust, further burning him. The stretch felt like it was almost tearing him apart. He said nothing, just panted. Mishka reached under Ben, grabbing his nip rings and twisting them until Ben jerked from the mix of pain and pleasure.

"Ben, are you okay?"

"I've never been happier. I have the man I love in my bed."

"Every weekend we'll be here, Benjie.'

"Oh you're back to calling me Benjie."

297

"You made me so happy today. I love you even more because you told me what you need and don't need to make you happy."

Mishka pounded his hole, igniting a desperate need. Once again, Mishka brushed his prostate, which made him shudder throughout. He rocked in time with Mishka, trying to accept his cock as deep as possible. Mishka reached around for Ben's cock, stroking it with his lubed fingers. He pounded him harder and harder, Ben's head buried in the sheets. Mishka rammed his cock in and out with intense speed and force. The more he banged, the better Ben felt, then he raised his butt even higher.

"You know how to make me come, you little tease."

Ben was exhausted when Mishka flooded the inside of his condom, setting off his own orgasm, both of them grunting and moaning. Ben's cum had been fucked out of him. The huge dick that was pounding his butt had slowly withdrawn, leaving behind a cold, empty feeling. Ben could still feel the sting on his butt cheeks from the hard slaps Mishka had given him while he viciously fucked him.

Mishka removed Ben's cuffs, rolled Ben on his side, and wrapped his arms around him.

"Making love to you is worth all the money in the world."

298

"I wanted this the moment you left me in the hotel."

"You're mine. Please don't leave me anymore. I can't take it."

"I'm sorry, Mishka. I didn't explain myself better."

"I'm sorry I left you without trying to understand why you wanted to go home."

"It's the weekend, are you staying here with me?" Ben asked.

"Damn right I am. I have my things in the limo downstairs." Mishka sent a text to his driver and Jasha.

They took a shower and dressed then returned to the patio and sat with water.

About five minutes later, the doorbell rang, both of them went to answer it.

The driver had two suitcases and he placed them next to the doorway. Kylan and Jasha were behind him.

"So, everything is okay here?" Kylan asked.

Mishka put his arm around Ben. "They are."

"Well, then Kylan and I are leaving for the weekend."

"Have fun. I'm moving in with Jasha, so we'll all be in New York soon," Kylan said.

"Wow, things are moving fast for you two," Ben said.

"We can move your things if you tell me what to pack," Kylan said.

"Thanks."

After dinner, Mishka and Ben left the condo and walked along the sand, getting their feet wet.

"Why didn't you answer my message last week?" Ben asked.

"I didn't understand why you wanted to go home, so I figured there wasn't anything more to say. I wanted you with me every night in my bed and you wanted to be here without me."

"Want to help me pack?" Ben asked.

"Are you sure you want to do this? I can't take you leaving me again," Mishka asked.

"I'm never leaving you."

"Let's go inside so I can kiss you," Mishka said.

BRINA BRADY

CHAPTER TWENTY-NINE

Mishka

After two weeks of living in New York City during the week and spending time at Ben's Wildwood condo on the weekends, things between them worked out better than Mishka had thought. Ben spent his days at the LGBTQ homeless shelter while Mishka worked at getting things legal in all aspects of his businesses. Jasha went to work with Mishka and Kylan went to the shelter with Ben. All in all, they were working out.

That evening, Mishka had promised Ben he'd go over some of his rules if he wanted to be his sub. Mishka decided to have this discussion in his office so he could have Ben fill out some papers. Dressed in one of his work suits, Mishka entered the room and stopped to kiss his excited Ben. He straightened out the black and gray stripped blanket draped over the back of the black leather sofa before sitting behind his desk. Ben stood near the fireplace with bookshelves on either side and picked up the Russian weapon on the mantel.

"Why do you have this old weapon on display?" Ben asked.

"That belonged to my grandfather who fought in the Russian Revolution. He gave it to me when I had visited him in Russia."

"Did you ever use it?" Ben asked.

"No. I display it to show my respect to my grandfather. Nothing else. It's not loaded with ammunition or anything like that."

"I've never seen a weapon like this one, and I've seen tons of them. My father collects old weapons."

"I didn't know Sal collected weapons, but nothing about him ever surprises me."

"Did you know he served in the army for four years?"

"He did?" Mishka couldn't imagine Sal taking orders from anyone.

"Yes. He never talks about it, but my grandfather told me."

"Sit down so we can begin," Mishka ordered.

Ben sat on one of the two padded chairs positioned in front of the desk. Mishka removed a folder from his side drawer and set it down. He pulled out the submissive checklist and pushed it across the desk to Ben.

"This is the sub checklist. Only check those items and activities you're interested in. At any time, you can change your mind if it doesn't work out for you. Check with honesty and desire." Mishka passed a pen to Ben.

Ben pushed his hair out of his eyes and picked up a black pen. "I will, Sir."

"Good."

Ben began ticking off things like no tomorrow, and when he was done, he handed it to Mishka. Ben had checked all the spanking implements which surprised Mishka. He was okay with all types of bondage except gags and full-face hoods. He also marked all the alternative punishments such as corner time, revocation of privileges, and writing lines. He left scat, water play, and a few other things unchecked. He wrote *red* for his safeword.

"That's an impressive list. As I told you before, the arrangement is between us. That means we decide what we want. I don't want you to be my sub twenty-four hours seven days a week. I want us to begin with evenings for scenes in the playroom, but I expect you to follow my rules throughout the day. I've listed a few rules. I'm going to read them to you and tell me if you can or can't follow them." Mishka pulled another paper from the folder.

"I know how to read," Ben said.

"Is that how you address me?" Mishka raised his voice.

304

"I know how to read, Sir."

"That's better, but since I make the decisions, I'll decide who reads what."

Ben's expression displayed one of painted tolerance. He had no idea what submission was in every situation, but Mishka would teach him to know his place, even though he was a brilliant man, who thought he had known everything about everything. And he pretty much did know about everything except he didn't understand everything about submission. Time would tell if he was serious about it.

"Yes, Sir."

"I have only a few rules. Please listen."

"Yes, Sir." Ben sat up straighter in his chair.

"Be respectful, loyal, honest, monogamous, and follow my orders. Your purpose is to serve, obey, and please me. If you break the rules, I'll punish you. Can you agree to my rules and consequences?" Mishka asked.

"When you say you'll punish me for breaking a rule, are you talking about whipping me with a belt?"

"Not necessarily. Some broken rules may not warrant that. I have other means of punishing you."

"Can you explain what other means of punishing are to me?"

305

"I'll use your list to guide me with your punishments. The spanking implements you've checked off can and will be used on you during punishment. At no time will anything unchecked be used. Can I have a yes or no answer?"

"Yes, Sir. I agree to your rules and consequences." Ben gave him a smile, sending Mishka's pulse racing. They had come so far from the first day they met in the alley. Ben had never regretted choosing Mishka over his family. His life would have meaning with a completeness he had always strived for.

"When we use the playroom, I'll usually send you in first. You're to remove all clothes, kneel, palms face up on your knees, and your head lowered. Can you do this? Yes or no?"

"Yes, Sir."

"Do you have any questions?" Mishka asked.

"Are you sure those are the only rules, Sir?"

"Anything not said will fall under obey my orders. You can suggest anything, but remember I have the last word."

"Do I have any jobs here?"

"No. You have a job and school. I won't come between your education or your work."

"Thank you, Sir."

"When you're collared, you'll wear it in the playroom and at BDSM clubs only. I don't want you wearing it to school or work. Our sexual lifestyle is private so don't flaunt it in public. You can discuss it with Kylan or Jasha if you want."

"When will you collar me?"

"Now, but we can celebrate with Kylan and Jasha on the weekend when we're in Wildwood."

"I'm really excited now." Ben's eyes teared a bit.

"Me, too."

"Do you have any hard limits, Sir?"

"Yes, I do. Do you want me to read my list?" Mishka asked.

"Yes, Sir."

Mishka logged on his laptop, searched for the list, and printed it out. "Pay attention."

"1. No scat, blood, or watersports play.

2. No public humiliation.

3. No photography or video without your permission.

4. Never punish you when I'm angry.

5. Never share you. So, what do you think of my hard limits?"

"Your limits make me feel safer."

"I prepared a contract between us. We can upgrade it at any time." Mishka signed the contract. Then he handed it back to Ben, who read and signed it. Mishka filed it in the folder and put it into his file cabinet.

"Let's check out the playroom."

"Thank you, Sir."

Mishka felt his heart turn when he saw the happiness in Ben's eyes. Mishka could literally feel his smile come on his own lips. Their eyes met when Ben's smile widened. He led Ben to the distant wing and unlocked the door to the playroom. It smelled like leather and polish. The large space had two smaller rooms off the main room. Shelves filled with all sorts of toys covered one wall. Immediately, Ben's attention went to the green chair against the wall. He did a double take when he saw the sign on it, which read *Ben's chair.* The furniture was scattered around the room and everything smelled so new. Mishka had rearranged the furniture and made the sign for the chair when Ben was sleeping. His eyes caught the new the St. Andrew's Cross they had stained together.

"Strip for me. Fold your clothes and put them on the bench." Mishka pointed to the bench on the far side of the room.

Ben slowly unzipped his jeans, the way he had in the alley, and Mishka loved every minute of his little strip tease. He proceeded to unbuckle his belt while Mishka eyed his every move. Ben pushed them to his ankles and stepped out of them at a faster pace. Then he whipped off his shirt. He proceeded to fold everything and place it all on the bench.

"You're teasing my cock." Mishka placed his hand on his erection.

"I wanted to give you pleasure, Sir."

"Read the rules to me." Mishka pointed to the poster.

"Rules for Playroom:

1. Do not speak without permission.

2. Enter, strip down, and kneel in the middle of the room.

3. Use safeword when needed.

4. Clean playroom and toys after each session."

"Kneel in the middle of the room the way I told you."

"Yes, Sir."

"I have to get something from our room. Stay here and think about your purpose and place in our relationship."

When Mishka went to the bedroom, his phone rang.

"There's a problem with Tony Banetti. He's still selling shit. He was told to leave so the bouncer kicked him out," Jasha said.

"Maybe someone needs to teach him a lesson once and for all."

"I'll take care of it," Jasha said.

This was part of the job Mishka didn't want to deal with, but he had to do it. His goal to clean up his clubs taxed him more than he wanted to admit. At some point, he'd become his father if he didn't stop certain elements from destroying his dream.

CHAPTER THIRTY

Ben

While Ben knelt there, his knees throbbed. He must have been waiting for Mishka for quite a while. He'd been lost in his own thoughts. Why was it taking Mishka so long? He wondered if Mishka's delay was deliberate, leaving him here in the playroom on his knees. Mishka had ordered him to think about his purpose and place. He didn't need any more time for his mind to do its normal circling around the same thoughts again and again. This dragged on too long for Ben's liking. He wasn't a patient man. He had a feeling that Mishka would be teaching him all about patience.

The door squeaked opened and Mishka entered the room wearing jeans and a T-shirt. Apparently, he had changed his clothes and must have taken a shower too for the amount of time Ben had been waiting.

"I have something for you, Ben." He cupped Ben's chin, lifting his head to face him and handed him a gold box.

"Thank you, Sir."

"Open it."

Ben gasped with delight when he removed the box top—a black leather collar engraved with his name, gleaming with diamond studs sparkled under the light.

"Wow, I love it. Thank you, Sir." Ben's eyes filled with tears. He quickly fisted them away.

"I made it myself especially for you," Mishka said.

"You are so creative and I love that you put part of you in the things we play with."

Reaching out, Mishka placed the collar around Ben's neck and clasped it. He looked into Ben's eyes with love and approval. He had come through with his promise after Ben had complained he hadn't been taking Ben's request to be his sub seriously.

"Ben, by placing this collar around your neck, I promise to keep you safe, teach you to grow, and to respect the needs of our relationship. I'll never violate your trust in me. This collar is a symbol that you're mine."

He kissed Ben's lip, leaving a trace of warmth on his lips.

"This collar means so much to me, Sir."

"I know it does and it means a great deal to me too. Would you like me to mark you to seal our relationship?"

"Yes, Sir." Ben had read about marking and knew it would leave a mark on him—although not a permanent one. He wanted to belong to Mishka in every way possible.

"To make it special, I'd like to put a male chastity device on you during the process as a symbol of your submission. Are you okay with that?" Mishka asked.

"I've never worn one, Sir. I'm willing to try it." Mishka wanted to lock his cock up. Ben hoped he didn't regret this. Well, if he did, he could safeword out of it.

Mishka went to the shelf area and picked up a new cock-cage in a package. He ripped it open and showed Ben what it looked like.

"Your penis will never reach its rock-hard erection so long as you're wearing this."

"So, this thing guarantees my cock will be denied an orgasm, right?"

"As long as you're wearing it, but later, who knows what will happen?"

Mishka smiled at him while he slid the cage over Ben's cock, snapped the lock, and put the key on a long chain around his neck. Ben looked down in horror.

The weight of the cage felt great and it was very solid and secure, but there wasn't any escape. It was very exciting, in a restricted way, to feel everything locked up so securely and without too much discomfort.

"I don't want you distracted during the marking. I'll keep the key around my neck. At any time, you can safeword out of it and I'll remove it instantly."

"Yes, Sir." Ben stared at the metal cage around his cock. He'd put his cock in jail.

"Follow me. I'm going to put you on the spanking bench and a pillow under you during the marking. Is that okay, Ben?"

"Yes, Sir."

"Go to the spanking bench."

Following Mishka's orders, Ben made his way to the bench and wondered which implement Mishka would mark him with since there were several of them hanging on the hooks in the room. Mishka placed a soft pillow on the bench for his cock cage to rest on.

"Face down on the bench."

"Yes, Sir." Ben carefully bent over the bench. "My cock can't stretch, Sir."

"If it hurts too much, use your safeword." Mishka made sure all was arranged properly, then returned to checking implements.

"Yes, Sir."

Mishka returned and placed a green bandana around Ben's eyes, ensuring he couldn't see anything.

"Drop your hands over the sides of the bench." Mishka strapped his wrists to the bench.

Ben jerked at the sound of the click. Every little sound freaked him out. Mishka had secured him on a spanking bench in the past, but today was different...and special. Mishka rubbed his hands up and down Ben's legs so lightly it tickled him.

"Tell me who I am to you."

"My Dom, Sir."

"I'm going to mark you to seal our bond."

"Umm... What are you going to mark me with, Sir?" His cock was demanding to swell, but the cage constricted him.

"I'm going to use a cane. Remember this isn't discipline. The marking is a reminder that you belong to me."

"Yes, Sir."

"If you accept your marking, I might allow you to come." Mishka licked the back of his balls.

"Fuck, Mishka. I can't get hard, let alone come, when you're making me crazy licking me like that."

316

"Is that how you address your Dom?" He pinched Ben's balls.

"No, Sir. Sorry, Sir."

Mishka dropped a feather light kiss on his ass. "Mmm your ass belongs to me. Do you understand?"

"Yes, Sir."

Ben heard Mishka walk over to the wall of hanging spanking implements and wondered which cane he'd choose. He hoped he could deal with the pain. The thing was he loved the pain, but he wouldn't be able to enjoy it with this damn cage.

"Ben, I'm going to use my cane on you. It will sting. You checked off the cane, right?" Mishka asked.

"Yes, Sir." Mishka had already known what he had checked off so he was double-checking in case Ben had changed his mind within the last thirty minutes.

"Have you ever been caned before?"

"No, Sir."

"It hurts like hell, but it will mark quickly and lasts longer. Ready?"

"Yes, Sir."

"Don't move." Mishka secured the straps to his ankles.

"No, Sir."

317

Mishka ran his hand gently over his ass. "Are you ready?"

"Yes, Sir." His voice trembled from fear and anticipation. He had no idea how hard Mishka would strike the cane against his bare ass.

Mishka slammed the cane down on his ass. Ben remained quiet. Fuck, this hurts. The cane sliced into his skin. He clenched his ass cheeks, preparing for the next blow.

The second one came down harder, but thankfully below the first strike. Ben had a difficult time breathing evenly.

Number three struck him right below where the second strike had landed.

Tears rolled down from under his blindfold from the pain and the horrifying sound the cane made against his ass.

Fuck. Fuck. Fuck. This hurts. Mishka set the cane on the bench.

It was over. He sighed with relief that he didn't make a fool out of himself.

"You're mine, boy," Mishka whispered in his ear. "I'm so proud of you."

Mishka untied the blindfold and set it on the bench, then unfastened the leather straps from his wrists and ankles. He helped Ben stand up and led him to the tiny room with a full-sized bed in it.

"Lie on your stomach."

Ben rested on his stomach on the bed. Mishka put some cream on his markings—whatever it was it removed some of the stinging.

"Turn over, Ben."

When he turned over and sat up, he groaned a little from the stinging.

Mishka handed him a bottle of cold water. "Drink this."

Ben was thirsty and drank most of it as fast as he could.

"Would you like some chocolate?"

"Yes, Sir. But my cock wants to come." Ben needed to come or he was going to go insane soon. He'd never deprived his cock of coming before.

Mishka handed him a bar of chocolate. "Eat this."

Ben ate the bar and drank more water. His cock was throbbing inside the cage.

"Now rest your head on the pillow, hands on the headboard, and lift your ass up for me."

319

Ben held on to the headboard, lowered his head on the pillow, and pushed his ass out as instructed.

First, Mishka ripped off his shirt, then shoved his jeans and briefs to his ankles and tossed them across the room. He slipped a lubed condom on his erection, climbed onto the bed, and knelt behind Ben's ass.

"You have such a pretty ass, Ben." Mishka kissed it.

Mishka rammed his cock inside Ben. He didn't expect Mishka to move so fast. As Mishka moved inside, he kept hitting Ben's prostate. Having Mishka inside of him after his marking felt glorious.

"Fuck me harder, Sir," Ben begged.

"I determine the pace, not you."

"Sorry, Sir," Ben said, gasping.

Mishka increased the speed as he pounded his ass. The long grueling thrusts ignited Mishka to explode his cum inside his condom.

"Are you frustrated, Ben?" Mishka slipped his cock out of Ben's ass and removed the condom. He threw it in a small trashcan while poor Ben was moaning. He returned and lubed a butt plug and inserted it in Ben's ass.

"I need to come, Sir." Ben's cock was suffering, unable to stretch or come.

Mishka flipped Ben over and unlocked his cock-cage, setting it on the bed stand.

"You've been a good boy, Ben. And good boys deserve to come."

Mishka kneeled on the bed between Ben's legs. Mishka reached for Ben's thighs, pulling him closer. He took Ben's cock in his mouth and began sucking for the first time. No one had ever made Ben feel like this before. It felt so damn good when Mishka's tongue raced up and down his shaft. He spent some time on the head, doing tongue swirls around it. His hands massaged Ben's balls. He stuck his tongue inside Ben's slit, jamming it in and out repeatedly.

Ben took a deep breath and said, "I'm going to come, Sir." He warned Mishka, so he could remove Ben's pulsing cock from his mouth, but he didn't. Mishka sucked harder. Finally, Ben couldn't hold his orgasm off any longer, and shot cum right into Mishka's mouth.

Ben moaned and made all kinds of loud noises while Mishka continued to suck him and swallow his cum. He licked Ben's cock clean.

"Ready for bed, Ben?"

Ben nodded.

Mishka scooped him up into his arms and tossed him over his shoulder. He carried him to the bedroom, and slid Ben under the covers on the bed.

"I loved what we did tonight," Ben said.

"Me too. You're such a turn on for me. Your body. Your voice. Did I say your ass?"

BRINA BRADY

CHAPTER THIRTY-ONE

Ben

Ben stopped at the jewelers to pick up an engraved bracelet for Mishka. From there, he walked to Banetti Ristorante to check on the new employee plus he had invited Mishka here for dinner. As soon as he walked into the restaurant, Marianna greeted him. Some of the others did too. He wasn't sure how he would be received him since his father had disowned him, but his grandfather had left him this restaurant and he would keep it in the family out of respect for him. "I'm sorry your mother left your father," Marianna said.

"She had her reasons. He's not an easy man to live with," Ben said.

"Is she returning to New Jersey?"

"I don't know, but you can call her." Ben wrote down her number on the back of his business card and handed it to her. "She'd love to hear from you."

Once he met with the new employee, he sat down with a glass of wine at a table and waited for Mishka. When he finally arrived, he looked like he had worked hard. They never discussed his family business and agreed to keep Ben out of it. But something was upsetting him by look on his face and Ben wanted to know. Mishka never asked for loyalty to his family, but what if he had to choose where his loyalty was.

"How was your day?" Ben asked as Mishka settled into his seat, but he wasn't expecting Mishka to share his problems with him.

"I'm beat from the shitty day I had. How was your day?"

"Sorry your day turned out bad. Mine was pretty good. I got accepted into a case study with my professor. We'll mostly be working the afternoons so I can work at the LGBTQ homeless shelter in the mornings. I'm really excited about it." Ben poured wine into Mishka's glass. He looked like he needed some relief.

"Thanks, Ben." Mishka sipped his wine. "You're so lucky you managed to get away from the family business. I sometimes envy you."

"It wasn't my choice to be disowned and even when I wasn't, they didn't want me in any leadership position. I wasn't welcomed in the family business because I was gay." Ben hurt just thinking of the constant rejection of his family each time. All because he was gay. Why should that

325

make a difference? They regarded him as half a man, another hurt he'd never get over.

"That's true, but you were able to pick a profession you wanted. I didn't get to choose what I wanted to do."

"What profession would you have chosen if you had a choice?" Ben asked.

"I wanted to be a teacher and still do. I went to college and studied business because that's what my father needed me to know for working with him. I did it to please him. But I still want to be a teacher," Mishka said.

"Where did you go to school?"

"Saint John's University. I commuted. I didn't get to go away to college."

"My father was only too glad to send me away."

"Did you fuck around and have fun?"

"No. I studied nonstop. I didn't have much time for anything else."

"I can see that, Ben. You're brilliant and you want to spend your time saving people instead of killing them." Mishka's eyes teared up.

"Breaking away from your parents is always difficult, but if you want something in your life you have to go for it. You love your father more than you care about your future plans. I think you have a great father, but I also think if you would have told him what you wanted, he might have helped you attain it. There are always family members to run the business." Ben could see the pain in Mishka's eyes. He must have had to deal with something that compromised him in some way, and he'd never confide in Ben which saddened him.

"You think so?" Mishka asked.

"I don't see anything in your father that wouldn't want you to be totally happy in life."

"It's too late for me to teach now," Mishka said.

"No, it's not. My professor told me he used to run his family medical supply store until he was forty-five. He went to school and did the requirements needed and now he's a professor. He still owns the store, but he hired a cousin to take over."

"That's an uplifting story." Mishka smiled for the first time since he sat down.

"Are you going to tell me what happened today?"

"I can't tell you. Let's just say it turned my stomach, but being in my position, it had to be done to move forward."

"Does it have to do with my family?" Ben asked, concerned.

Mishka raised his eyebrows. "Ben, I want to keep you out of my business because you're still a Banetti and not a Chernov. You have no loyalty to my family."

"I may be a Banetti, but I'm no longer associated with my family."

"What about your mother?"

"Well, she's a Banetti by marriage. And yes, I'm still talking to my mother."

"You have aunts, uncles, and cousins. What about them?"

"I haven't contacted any of them and have no plans to do so."

"Who are these employees in your restaurant?" Mishka turned to look at Ben's cousin, Marianna.

"Oh, I guess I do have some family members working here." Ben didn't realize he was still very connected to the Banetti family. He certainly had no plans to fire anyone to prove he had no loyalty to them because in a way he was very much associated with them. Basically, it was just his father he didn't see and not by choice.

"If and when you want to know what I do, you must dissociate from all Banetti family members and pledge your loyalty to the Chernovs. I don't think you're in that place now."

328

"You're right. I'm sorry I asked. I just thought I could help you in some way."

"You being here with me has helped more than you'll ever know. I'm glad we're back together. Are you happy with our relationship?" Mishka asked.

"Yes, of course. I love being with you every night. My life never had such meaning and happiness. You make everything I do special. You should know that I do love the Chernovs."

"And how about Mishka Chernov, do you love him too?" Mishka grinned.

"I love you, Mishka Chernov, so much that I left my family over you. That's how much I love you."

Mishka pulled a box out of his pocket and handed it to Ben. "Open it, I bought it for you."

Ben opened the gift and inside was a gold chain engraved on the inside. It read, *To Ben, Love Mishka.*

"I love it. This really means a lot. I want to wear it every day."

"I was hoping you would. It's an outward symbol we belong to each other."

"It's like a collar in a way."

"It's more than a collar. You're much more than a sub to me. It means I love you, Ben."

Ben handed a gift from his pocket to Mishka. "I bought you something too."

Mishka opened it and inside was a diamond-studded leather bracelet. Inside the bracelet, it read, *I love you, Mishka*."

"This is perfect. This bracelet says it all. Thank you."

"What are you going to order?" Ben asked.

"Since this is your restaurant, you order for me."

"I'll surprise you."

"You always do."

The End

BRINA BRADY

ABOUT THE AUTHOR

I am from Huntington Beach, Ca. I taught various subjects at a Continuation High School in Los Angeles, California for 27 years. I obtained a Bachelor's of Arts Degree in History, Secondary Social Science Credential, and a Master's Degree in Secondary Reading and Secondary Education from California State University, Long Beach. I also enrolled in some creative writing classes at UCLA.

BRINA BRADY

Connect With Brina Brady

I would love to hear from my readers, so please drop me a line.

My email address:

mailto:brinabrady@gmail.com

Join my Reader's Group here:

https://www.facebook.com/groups/146904702344189/

Please visit my WordPress Blog here:

http://brinabrady.wordpress.com

Friend me on Facebook here:

https://www.facebook.com/brina.brady.3

Follow me on Twitter here:

https://twitter.com/BrinaBrady

Follow me on BookBub here:

https://www.bookbub.com/authors/brina-brady

Follow me on Pinterest here:

http://www.pinterest.com/brinabrady/

Follow me on Instagram:

https://www.instagram.com/bradybrina/

Follow Me on Liker

https://www.liker.com/brina148770/wall

OTHER BOOKS

RENT ME SERIES 1-5

"Rent Me" by Brina Brady (Book 1)

http://www.amazon.com/Rent-Me-Book-ebook/dp/B00KLNSLBQ/

Russian mobster spanks his rent boy. Ouch!

Rent Boy Brennen wants to belong to his lover Dmitri Dubrovsky. The Russian mobster controls every inch of his life in and out of bed. Brennen works for Dmitri's escort service. His only desire is to please his lover. When Dmitri marries Nika, his lover moves him out of their home to an apartment in Beverly Hills and tells him nothing has changed.

What is Brennen going to do now?

Brennen does not understand his lover's Russian culture not allowing homosexuality. Two different cultures and age difference clash.

"Own Me" by Brina Brady (Book 2)

http://www.amazon.com/dp/B00VDQLDZ6/

"Make Me" by Brina Brady (Book 3)

http://www.amazon.com/dp/B016B6MZZY/

"For Me" by Brina Brady (Book 4)

http://www.amazon.com/Me-Christmas-Story-Rent-ebook/dp/B018PWUVFI/

"Find Me" by Brina Brady (Book 5)

https://www.amazon.com/Find-Me-Rent-Book-ebook/dp/B01MT9S6PD/

BEND OVER SERIES 1-4
"Bend Over" by Brina Brady (Book 1)

http://www.amazon.com/Bend-Over-Book-ebook/dp/B00P2XO5YM/

Runaway 18-year-old Shane O'Rourke is living under the Huntington Beach Pier.

He carries many secrets from his past. Shane wasn't allowed to explore his sexuality when he lived home with his father, The Reverend. His submissive nature and desires had to remain fantasies.

Shane meets a dark stranger on the beach. Julien Callier is a Dom from Martinique and is sixteen years older than Shane. Bad boy Shane wants to win the heart of Julien Callier and become his sub. But does he really understand what Julien expects from his boy?

Julien's heart goes out to this gorgeous boy and he takes him under his wing, grooming him to be his sub. Julien is determined to let Shane experience the good life, even financing his education, but he's challenged at every turn by Shane's rebellious nature.

When Shane's defiant behavior threatens to come between them for good, Julien has to act fast to teach Shane the meaning of real submission.

Can Julien tame the bad boy? Can Shane give up his old ways of stealing, lying, and using drugs? The playroom is open.

"Don't Throw Me Away" by Brina Brady (Book 2)

http://www.amazon.com/gp/product/B0117VIQW4/

"Spanked in the Woodshed" by Brina Brady (Book 3)

https://www.amazon.com/Spanked-Woodshed-Bend-Over-Book-ebook/dp/B01BOEWBB6

"Breaking Roadblocks" by Brina Brady (Book 4)

https://www.amazon.com/gp/product/B07649W6RF

IRISH RUNAWAY SERIES 1-3
"The Runaway Gypsy Boy" by Brina Brady (Book 1)

https://www.amazon.com/Runaway-Gypsy-Boy-Irish-Book-ebook/dp/B01FIFE3Q8/

Twenty-year-old Daniel Serban loses his dancing job and threats of being outed to his family force him to flee Limerick, Ireland. Daniel fears his father and the other gypsy men will force him to marry his betrothed, or bring bodily harm to him for being gay.

As chance would have it, he ends up in Cleary's Pub, a gay leather bar in Galway where he meets the grouchy, ginger-bear Ronan O'Riley. Daniel had no idea how much meeting the Dom would transform his life.

Ronan O'Riley has been unable to move on since the death of his sub a year ago, that is until a troubled gypsy boy steps into Cleary's. Ronan's lonely existence is about to change.

Can Ronan convince Daniel to trust him or will Daniel's fears of his past ruin any chance of a relationship? Unexpected heated attraction in the barn ignites their relationship to move forward. Though the two men have many of the same dreams, Daniel's secrets and Ronan's need to gain Daniel's trust are just a few of the many challenges they must overcome if they are to be together.

"Master Cleary's Boys" by Brina Brady (Book 2)

https://www.amazon.com/Master-Clearys-Boys-Irish-Runaway-ebook/dp/B01M0AF8DR/

"Master Braden's Houseboy" by Brina Brady (Book 3)

https://www.amazon.com/dp/B07HX2HR3G

BURIED SECRETS SERIES
"Buried Secrets" by Brina Brady (Book 1)

https://www.amazon.com/dp/B07MGHSFQS

When Alek Belanov loses his family at four years old, his Russian mobster uncle raises him.

Now, at twenty-two, Alek wants nothing more than to find out who murdered his family and why. After Alek gets out of prison for a crime he didn't commit, his uncle sends him away to the Gay Protection Society, claiming Alek's life is in danger.

Sexy Rafe Escobar is the head of the secret Gay Protection Society, and he chooses Alek as his personal charge. Rafe warns Alek that if he breaks security rules, he will discipline him. Alek has some slip-ups here and there, but he adores his protector and wishes to please him in every way.

Alek quickly finds his place among the other men who seek shelter and those who guard them. What was supposed to be a safe haven becomes a group on the run as security breaches and threats force them to move from town to town.

Is Rafe and Alek's relationship strong enough to withstand the secrets and deceptions of people trying to destroy them?

"Taming Emilio" by Brina Brady (Book 2)

https://www.amazon.com/gp/product/B07TYS81F2

STANDALONES

"Cabin Commotion" by Brina Brady

https://www.amazon.com/dp/B079Y29G5V/

Playboy Blaze is the son of Sal Bossio, a New York City Italian mobster. His father orders him to his Vermont cabin for one month while he settles mob business. Blaze hires a rent boy for one month, but unexpected events occur, and he finds himself alone in Vermont. When he reaches his cabin, he finds a stranger sleeping in his bed. The gorgeous gingered-haired man could be a hitman sent by his father's enemies.

High-paid escort Marcus graduates college and he's ready to leave The Manor. Working for pimp Kalepo for four years, Marcus believes there's no way out without paying a fatal price. Marcus leaves California on a train to New York City and a bus to a rented Vermont cabin for one month to hide from Kalepo.

Two lonely men solve the cabin commotion by sharing the only bed in the cabin during their sex fest saving hidden pasts and tough decisions until the month ends.

"Sir Ethan's Contract" by Brina Brady

https://www.amazon.com/dp/B07DZ18WZ7

Rich, intelligent, and ridiculously sexy, Sir Ethan finds his submissive left him, breaking their D/s contract. Not wanting to be alone, Sir Ethan places an ad, offering a large sum of money for a submissive man. He wants to take care of a submissive, make rules, and dish out the consequences.

American born Adrien Dubois loses his family when ICE deports them to France. He hooks up with a mean ex-felon in a dilapidated trailer. When Stone abandons him, Adrien finds an ad for a submissive.

Sir Ethan is going to be Adrien's Dominant for one month, and he'll make lots of money. What could go wrong? He's going to take care of Adrien, and all he has to do is follow Sir Ethan's rules or his Dominant will spank him. Adrien is terrified to admit it, deep down he knows that soon he'll beg Sir Ethan to strip him bare and teach Adrien what happens to bad boys.

Two men dumped not looking for love, one needs money, and the other wants convenient sex.

"Leather Paddles" by Brina Brady

https://www.amazon.com/Leather-Paddles-Brina-Brady-ebook/dp/B082FVS7LP/

He's had it with Doms. Never again…but maybe this one is different.

Twenty-two-year-old Jesse finds himself abandoned by his abusive Dom after four years in an unhappy BDSM relationship. Devastated, he moves in with his best friend, Charlie, and his Dom. He attends college and works in the university library. He doesn't have time nor plans to look for another Dom.

Master Andrew, the owner of BDSM club Leather Paddles, lost his husband five years ago. Ever since, he plays with different subs and is perfectly happy to leave it with that. He doesn't want another boy to call his own.

Once Master Andrew meets Jesse, things click for both of them, but Jesse remains skittish about getting involved with anyone. However, Master Andrew comes up with a plan to rein Jesse in his playroom and his heart.

Other people keep interfering, trying to separate the couple. Are Master Andrew and Jesse up to the challenge to move forward to their happily ever after?

Leather Paddles is a stand-alone MM romance featuring an insecure boy and a strict but caring Master. It has BDSM elements and a guaranteed HEA.

"Baby Bear" by Brina Brady

https://www.amazon.com/dp/B0893L5694/

Abel's heartbreaking childhood contributes to his emotional baggage; his life has been one of hate, denial, and secrecy. His father, a polygamist cult leader, sends young men away from the compound in Utah so at eighteen, his mother drives him to the city. A dancing job opportunity finds Abel moving to Minnesota. Two years later he's mysteriously fired. Without savings, Abel needs a Daddy to take care of him, and he's found the perfect one at the Blue Diamond Diner.

Diner owner Darius Eriksen's dream is to find a boy who needs a Papa Bear to take care of his needs. Darius belongs to the Bearded Papa Bears. Membership requires Papa Bears wanting to be a daddy to a boy; they pledge to love, care, and discipline their Baby Bear. Two years after Darius's Baby Bear leaves him for another Papa Bear, he's ready to find a new Baby Bear and commit again.

W is about two damaged souls, realizing that the other is exactly what they need at the right times of their lives. This story is a stand-alone MM romance that follows their relationship. It has some D/S elements and a guaranteed HEA.

Made in the USA
Middletown, DE
10 April 2021